AURÉLIA

AURÉLIA

BY GÉRARD DE NERVAL

TRANSLATED BY GEOFFREY WAGNER

& other writings translated by

ROBERT DUNCAN & MARC LOWENTHAL

DRAWINGS BY GENT STURGEON

E

EXACT CHANGE
BOSTON
1996

CONTENTS

PUBLISHER'S NOTE

Gérard de Nerval (the pseudonym of Gérard Labrunie, 1808-1855) belonged to a group of French literary eccentrics known in their time as *bousingos:* "rowdies" notorious for their orgies, for eating ice cream out of skulls, for holding literary seminars in the nude, for loudly playing musical instruments none of them knew how to play. But Nerval distinguished himself amongst such hijinks by going insane. Committed first in 1841, Nerval spent the rest of his life in and out of an asylum run by a Dr. Esprit Blanche, later by his son Émile. Nerval's *bousingo*-style eccentricities (the most famous being walking a lobster on a pale blue ribbon through the gardens of the Palais Royal) reached their conclusion when he hung himself from an apron string he called the garter of the queen of Sheba. Dr. Émile Blanche commented, *"Gérard de Nerval s'est pendu parce qu'il a vu sa folie face à face"* [Gérard de Nerval hung himself because he looked his madness in the face]. In his pockets were the final pages of his greatest work, *Aurélia ou Le Rêve et la Vie.*

Aurélia is Nerval's account of his descent into madness, a condition provoked in part (as Nerval explains it) by his unrequited passion for an actress, Jenny Colon. This document of dreams and obsession has fascinated artists such as Joseph Cornell, who cited passages from it in order to explain his own work; Antonin Artaud, who saw his madness mirrored by Nerval's; and André Breton, who placed Nerval in the highest echelon of Surrealist heroes.

In the "Manifesto of Surrealism," Breton commented that the group "could probably have taken over the word SUPERNATURALISM employed by Gérard de Nerval... It appears, in fact, that Nerval possessed to a tee the spirit with which we claim a kinship..." But it is interesting to note that Surrealism's official enthusiasm for Nerval seemed to take strongest hold with artists on the fringe of the group, those more alone rather than in the midst of Breton's collective campaigns. Cornell and Artaud fit this mold, as does the tragic spiritualist René Daumal. Daumal wrote a beautiful essay, "Nerval the Nyctalope," in which he declares that he and Nerval have occupied the same dream world; that, "Never will any book by my hand have the exact color of my blood, never will any book be so truly mine as *Aurélia*." Perhaps this best describes the response to the work felt by many of Nerval's admirers.

Geoffrey Wagner's translation of *Aurélia* was first published in 1957 by Grove Press in a volume called *Selected Writings*, reprinted by the University of Michigan Press in 1970. From that same volume we have reprinted Geoffrey Wagner's translation of *Sylvie*, the best known of the stories from Nerval's collection *Les Filles du Feu*, and the subject of a famously admiring essay by Marcel Proust. To these are added a group of works, newly translated by Marc Lowenthal, that help explicate some of Nerval's personal mythologies: *Octavie* and *Isis*, both from *Les Filles du Feu; Pandora*, a story at one time intended for that collection; and, as a bookend to *Aurélia*, the other major work from Nerval's last years, *Promenades et Souvenirs* [*Walks and Memories*]. Finally, we are pleased to be able to include Robert Duncan's translation of the magical cycle of poems, *Les Chimères* [*The Chimeras*], which Nerval also published in *Les Filles du Feu*; this with the kind permission of New Directions.

AURÉLIA

OR LIFE AND THE DREAM

PART ONE

I

Our dreams are a second life. I have never been able to penetrate without a shudder those ivory or horned gates which separate us from the invisible world. The first moments of sleep are an image of death; a hazy torpor grips our thoughts and it becomes impossible for us to determine the exact instant when the "I," under another form, continues the task of existence. Little by little a vague underground cavern grows lighter and the pale gravely immobile shapes that live in limbo detach themselves from the shadows and the night. Then the picture takes form, a new brightness illumines these strange apparitions and gives them movement. The spirit world opens before us.

Swedenborg called these visions *Memorabilia;* he owed them more often to musing than to sleep; *The Golden Ass* of Apuleius, Dante's *Divine Comedy,* are two poetic models of such studies of the human soul. Following their example I am going to try to describe the impressions of a long illness which took place entirely within the mysteries of my soul; I do not know why I use the word "illness," for as far as my physical self was concerned, I never felt better. Sometimes I thought my strength and energy were doubled, I seemed to know everything, understand everything. My imagination gave me infinite delight. In recovering what men call reason, do I have to regret the loss of those joys?...

This *Vita Nuova* had two phases for me. Here are the notes belonging to the first. A woman whom I had loved for a long while, and whom I shall call Aurélia, was lost to me. The circumstances of this event, which was to have such a great effect on my life, are of little importance. Each one of us can search his memory for the most heartrending emotion he has known, the most terrible blow that fate has inflicted on his soul. It is a question of deciding whether to go on living, or die. I will later explain why I did not choose death. Condemned by the woman I loved, guilty of a fault for which I could no longer hope for forgiveness, nothing was left to me but to throw myself into vulgar distractions. I affected gaiety and lack of concern. I traveled about the world, and was foolishly fascinated by variety and caprice. I fell in love with the costumes and curious habits of distant peoples, for it seemed to me that in this way I was changing the conditions of good and evil, the terms — so to speak — of what for us Frenchmen are the "feelings."

"What madness," I told myself, "to go on platonically loving a woman who no longer loves you. This is the evil result of your reading. You have taken the conceits of poets quite seriously and fashioned for yourself a Laura or a Beatrice out of an ordinary person of the present century... You'll forget her directly you start a new affair."

The dizzy whirl of a merry carnival in an Italian town dispelled all my melancholy ideas. I was so happy at the relief I felt that I informed all my friends of my joy and, in my letters, gave them as the permanent state of my spirit what was but a feverish overexcitement.

One day a very well known woman arrived in the town. She made friends with me and, accustomed as she was to giving an effect of both pleasure and brilliance, drew me without difficulty into the circle of her admirers. At the end of an evening during which she had been both simple and yet full of a charm that everyone had felt, I imagined myself so smitten by her that I wrote to her without waiting a moment. I was so happy to feel my heart capable of a new love!... In this artificial enthusiasm I borrowed the same forms of expression which, so short a while ago, I had used to declare a true and long-felt love. As soon as the letter had gone, I wanted to take it back, and in my solitude I dreamed over what seemed to me a profanation of my memories.

The next evening lent my new love the glamour of the night before. The lady showed herself affected by what I had written, being at the same time astonished by my sudden ardor. I had, in one day, gone through many stages of those feelings that a man can experience for a woman with sincerity. She confessed that my letter had surprised her and yet made her proud.

I tried to be convincing, but despite all I endeavored to say I could no longer attain the same high style of my letter in our talks, with the result that I was reduced to avowing — with tears in my eyes — that I had deceived myself and abused her. Perhaps my maudlin confidence had charm, however, for my vain protestations of affection were replaced by a friendship far stronger in its gentleness.

II

Later I met her in another town, where there was also the lady with whom I was hopelessly in love.[1] By chance they met each other, and there is no doubt that my new friend took the opportunity of softening towards me the one from whose heart I had been exiled. The result was that one day I found myself at the same party as her, and she came up to me, holding out her hand. How was I to interpret this action and the sad long look which accompanied her greeting? I imagined it meant forgiveness for the past. The divine accent of pity gave the simple words she addressed to me an indescribable value as though something religious had mingled with the sweetness of a love until then profane, and impressed upon it the quality of eternity.

An imperative duty compelled me to return to Paris, but I was firmly resolved not to stay there more than a few days and then to come back to my two friends. Joy and impatience induced in me a kind of giddiness which was aggravated by the business of having to settle my affairs. One evening, at about midnight, I was returning to the quarter where I lived, when I happened to raise my eyes and notice the number on a house, lit by a street-lamp. The number was that of my own age. As I looked down I saw in front of me a woman with hollow eyes, whose features seemed to me like Aurélia's. I said to myself: "I am being warned of either her death or mine." For some reason I decided on the latter of the two ideas, and had the impression that it would come about at the same time on the following day.

That night I had a dream which confirmed me in my belief.

I was wandering about a vast building composed of several rooms, some of which were given up to study, others to conversation or philosophical discussion. Rather interested I remained in one of the first of these, and thought I recognized my old instructors and fellow-students. The lessons on Greek and Latin authors went on in that steady hum which sounds like a prayer to the goddess Mnemosyne. I passed on into another room where the philosophical discussions were taking place. I took part in one for a while, then went to look for my own room in a sort of inn with gigantic staircases crowded with hurrying travelers.

I got lost several times in the long corridors and then, as I was going through one of the central galleries, I was struck by a strange sight. A creature of enormous proportions — man or woman I do not know — was fluttering painfully through the air and seemed to be struggling with heavy clouds. At last, out of breath and at the end of its strength, it collapsed into the middle of the dark courtyard, catching and crumpling its wings on the roofs and balustrades. For a moment I was able to observe it closely. It was colored with ruddy hues and its wings glittered with a myriad changing reflections. Clad in a long gown of antique folds, it looked like Dürer's *Angel of Melancholy.* I could not keep myself from crying out in terror and this woke me up with a start.

The next day I hurried to see all my friends. Mentally I said farewell to them and, telling them nothing of what was in my mind, I talked warmly on mystical matters. I surprised them by being particularly eloquent. It seemed to me as if I knew everything and that in those last moments of mine the mysteries of the world were being revealed to me.

That evening, as the fatal hour approached, I was seated with two of my friends round a table discussing painting and music, defining my idea of the generation of colors and the meaning of numbers. One of them, Paul, wanted to take me home, but I told him I was not going back.

"Where are you going?" he asked me.

"To the East."[2]

And, as he walked with me, I began searching the sky for a star I thought I knew as having some influence on my fate. When I had found it, I went on walking, following the streets from which it was visible, walking, as it were, towards my destiny, anxious to see the star up to the moment when death would strike me down.

When we had reached a junction of three streets, however, I refused to go any further. It seemed that my friend was employing superhuman strength to make me move. He grew larger in my eyes and took on the aspect of an Apostle. The spot on which we stood seemed to rise up and lose its urban appearance: on a hill, surrounded by enormous solitudes, that scene became a struggle between two spirits, like a Biblical temptation.

"No," I cried, "I don't belong to your heaven. Those in that star are waiting for me. They went before the revelation you have announced to me. Let me go to them, for the one I love belongs to them, and it is there we are to meet again."

III

Here began what I shall call the overflowing of the dream into real life. From that moment on, everything took on at times a double aspect — and did so, too, without my powers of reasoning ever losing their logic or my memory blurring the least details of what happened to me. Only my actions were apparently insensate, subject to what is called hallucination, according to human reason...

Many times the idea has occurred to me that in certain serious moments in life some Spirit of the outer world becomes suddenly embodied in the form of an ordinary person, and influences or tries to influence us without the individual in question having any knowledge of it or remembering anything about it.

Seeing that his efforts were useless, my friend had left me, no doubt imagining that I was prey to some obsession which the walk would calm away. When I found myself alone, I pulled myself together with an effort and set off again in the direction of the star, from which I had never removed my eyes. As I walked along I sang a mysterious hymn which I seemed to remember having heard in a previous existence, and which filled me with ineffable joy. At the same time I took off my terrestrial garments and scattered them about me. The roadway seemed to lead continually upwards and the star to grow bigger. Then I stood still, my arms outstretched, waiting for the moment when my soul should break free from my body, attracted magnetically by the rays of the star. A shudder went through me. Regret for the earth and for those I loved there gripped my heart, and so ardently within myself did I beseech the Spirit drawing me up towards it that it seemed as if I went down again among men. A night patrol surrounded me. I had the idea that I had grown very big and that since I was possessed of electrical forces I would overthrow all who approached me. There was something comic in the care I took to spare the strength and lives of the soldiers who had picked me up.

If I did not think that a writer's duty is to analyze with sincerity what he feels in grave moments of life, and if I had not in view to be useful, I would stop here, and make no attempt to describe my later experiences in a series of visions which were either insane or, vulgarly, diseased.

Stretched out on a camp bed, I thought I saw the sky unveil itself to me as if to make me full of remorse for having wished, with all the strength of my spirit, to step down again on the earth I was leaving... Immense circles took shape in infinity, like the orbs formed by water when something falls in and disturbs it. Each region was peopled with radiant faces and took on color, moved and melted in turn, and a Divinity, always the same, tossed away smiling the furtive masks of its various incarnations and at last imperceptibly took refuge in the mystic splendors of the Asiatic skies.

By one of those phenomena that everyone must have experienced in certain dreams, this celestial vision did not make me oblivious of what was going on around me. Lying on the camp bed, I heard the soldiers talking about some unknown person, who had been arrested like me, and whose voice had rung out in the same room. By a strange effect of vibration it felt as though his voice was echoing in my own chest, and that my soul was, so to speak, assuming a dual existence — distinctly divided between vision and reality. For a second I thought of making an effort to turn towards the person in question; then I shivered as I remembered a well-known German superstition which says that everyone has a *double* and that when you see him death is close at hand. I shut my eyes and went into a confused state of mind where the fantastic or real figures around me broke up into a thousand fugitive shapes. Once I saw by me two of my friends who were there reclaiming me: the soldiers pointed me out: then the door opened and someone of my build, whose face I could not see, went out with my friends to whom I called out vainly.

"But there's some mistake!" I cried. "They came for me and someone else has gone out."

I made so much noise that they put me in a cell.

For some hours I remained there in a sort of stupor: finally the two friends whom I imagined I had seen already came to fetch me in a carriage. I told them everything that had happened, but they denied having come during the night. I dined with them quite calmly. But as night approached, it seemed that I had to dread the same hour which, the day before, had nearly proved fatal to me. I asked one of them for an Oriental ring he wore on his finger, which I looked on as an ancient talisman. I took a scarf and knotted the ring around my neck, taking care to turn the stone, which was a turquoise, on to a place on the nape of my neck where I felt a pain.[3] I was convinced that it was through this spot that my soul would try to leave my body, at the moment when a certain ray from the star I had seen the night before coincided, in relation to myself, with its zenith. Either by chance, or as a result of my profound preoccupation, I fell down as though struck by a thunderbolt at the same time as on the evening before. I was put on a bed, and for a long time I lost the meaning and connection of images that came to me. This state lasted for several days. I was taken away to an asylum. Many of my friends and relations came to see me there without my being aware of it. The only difference as far as I was concerned between waking and sleeping was that in the former everything was transfigured in my eyes. Everyone who came near me seemed changed, material objects appeared in a dim penumbra that softened their shapes; shafts of light and the combinations of colors were distorted in such a way as to keep me in a constant series of interlinked impressions, whose credibility was continued in the dream state, more abstracted as it was from exterior elements.

IV

One evening I was positive I had been removed to the banks of the Rhine. In front of me were sinister rocks, their silhouettes dimly outlined in the gloom. I went into a cheerful house, where a ray from the setting sun cut through the green shutters which were festooned with vines. It appeared to me that I was

entering a house I knew well, belonging to one of my mother's uncles, a
Flemish painter who had been dead for more than a century. Half-finished
pictures hung here and there: one was of the famous water spirit of these
parts. An old woman servant, whom I called Marguerite and whom I seemed
to have known from infancy, said to me:

"Why don't you lie down on your bed? You've come a long way and your
uncle won't be in until late. We'll wake you up for supper."

I lay down on a fourposter bed whose drapes were decorated with large
red flowers. In front of me, hung on the wall, was a rustic clock and on this
clock was a bird which began to talk like a human being. I had the idea that
my grandfather's soul was in that bird, but I was no more astonished by his
new shape and speech than I was to find myself transported a century back.
The bird talked to me about living members of my family and of those who
had died at various times or other as if they were all contemporaries, and said
to me:

"You see your uncle took care to paint *her* portrait in advance... Now *she*
is with us."

I turned to a canvas of a woman dressed in an old German costume: she
was leaning over a river bank, her eyes fixed on a cluster of forget-me-nots.
Then little by little the darkness thickened and the shapes, sounds and the
feeling of places became confused in my sleepy spirit; I thought I was falling
into a chasm that crossed the world. I felt myself carried painlessly along on
a current of molten metal, and a thousand similar streams, the colors of
which indicated different chemicals, crisscrossed the breast of the world like
those blood vessels and veins that writhe in the lobes of the brain. They all
flowed, circulated and throbbed just like that, and I had a feeling that their

currents were composed of living souls in a molecular condition, and that the speed of my own movement alone prevented me from distinguishing them. A whitish light filtered bit by bit into these channels, and at last I saw spread out before me a new horizon like an enormous cupola in which were scattered islands surrounded by luminous waves. I found myself on a bright shore, in this sunless day, and I saw an old man tilling the earth. I recognized him as the man who had spoken to me through the bird's voice, and, either because he told me directly or because I understood it innately, it became clear to me that our ancestors take the forms of certain animals in order to visit us on earth, and that thus they are present as silent observers of the various phases of our existence.

The old man left his work and came with me to a house that stood nearby. The surrounding countryside reminded me of a part of Flanders where my parents lived and have their graves today. The hedged field skirting the wood, the neighboring lake, the river where the laundry is done, the village itself with its steep street, the hills of dark rock and their tufts of broom and heather — it was a rejuvenated image of the places I had loved. Only the house I went into was unknown to me. I understood it had existed in some former period, and that in this world I was now visiting the ghosts of material things accompanied those of human bodies.

I entered a large room where a crowd of people had gathered. On all sides I found faces I knew. The features of dead relations, whom I had mourned, were there reproduced in others who, clad in more ancient costumes, gave me the same paternal greeting.

They appeared to have collected for a family banquet. One of these relations came up and embraced me tenderly. He wore ancient clothes, the colors of which seemed to have faded, and his smiling face beneath his powdered hair somewhat resembled my own. He seemed to me to be more definitely alive than the others and, as it were, in closer contact with my own spirit. He was my uncle. He made me sit next to him and a kind of communication was established between us. I cannot say I heard his voice; only, as my thoughts settled on some question, the explanation immediately became clear to me, and images took distinct shape before my eyes like animated pictures.

"Then it's true," I exclaimed delightedly, "that we are immortal and retain here the replicas of the world we once inhabited. What happiness to think that everything we've loved will always exist around us!... I was very tired of life."

"Don't be too quick to rejoice," he said, "for you still belong to the world above and you have still to undergo hard years of trial. The abode that so delights you has itself its sorrows, its struggles, and its dangers. The earth on which we lived is still the theater where our destinies are woven and unraveled. We are the gleams of that central fire which gives it life and which is already growing weak..."

"What!" I cried. "Do you mean the earth could die and we be hurled into oblivion?"

"Oblivion," he answered, "does not exist in the sense it is understood, but the earth itself is a material body whose soul is the sum of the souls it contains. Matter can no more perish than mind, but it can be modified according to good and evil. Our past and future are intimately connected. We live in our race and our race lives in us."

This idea immediately became clear to me. The walls of the room seemed to open onto infinite perspectives and I saw an uninterrupted chain of men and women, in whom I was and who were myself: the costumes of every nation, visions of every country all appeared to me distinctly at the same time, as if my faculties of observation had been multiplied — and yet not muddled — by a phenomenon of space comparable to that of time, whereby a century of action is concentrated in a minute of dream. My amazement grew as I saw that this vast assembly was composed only of those people who were in the room, and whose shapes I had seen separating and combining in a thousand fugitive aspects.

"There are seven of us," I said to my uncle.

"That is, in fact," he replied, "the emblematic number of every human family and, by extension, seven times seven, and so on."*

This answer, which I cannot hope to make comprehensible, remains very obscure even to me. No metaphysical terms exist in which to express the perception which came to me then of the relationship between this conglomeration of people and universal harmony. In father and mother we can see the analogy of the electric forces of nature; but how can we establish the individual forces that emanate from them, and from which they themselves emanate, like the *face* of a collective cosmogony whose component elements are simultaneously multiple and limited? You might as well enquire of the flower why it has that number of petals or that number of divisions in its corolla... or the earth of the shapes it assumes, the sun of the colors it creates.

---

*Seven was the number of Noah's family; but one of the seven was mysteriously related to the previous generations of the Elohim!...[4] Imagination, in a lightning-flash, showed me the multiple gods of India like symbols of families as it were primitively concentrated. I fear to go further for there is also in the Trinity a terrible mystery... We are born under Biblical laws...

V

Everything around me changed its form. The spirit with whom I was talking no longer looked the same. He was now a youth who received ideas from me rather than vice versa... Had I traveled too far in these vertiginous heights? I seemed to understand that these questions were obscure and dangerous, even for the spirits of that world I now saw... Perhaps, too, some superior power forbade me those enquiries. I saw myself wandering through the streets of a busy, unknown city. I noticed that it was composed of many little hills and dominated by a mountain which was covered with houses. Among the inhabitants of this metropolis I distinguished certain men who appeared to belong to a special nation; their keen, determined air and energetic cast of countenance made me think of some independent warrior race from the mountains, or from some seldom-visited islands; and yet these men had managed to maintain their fierce individuality in the center of a large city and surrounded by a mixed population of ordinary people. Who were they? My guide made me climb up steep and noisy streets where the various sounds of industry could be heard. We went higher still by means of long flights of steps, beyond which the view opened out. Here and there were terraces clad in trellises, small gardens laid out on a few level spaces, roofs, lightly-built summer-houses painted and carved with fantastic patience: vistas linked together by long trains of climbing verdure seduced the eye and delighted the mind like a delicious oasis, a neglected solitude above the tumult and the noise below, which was here no more than a murmur. People often talk of outlawed races living in the shadows of some necropolis or catacomb; but here, there could be no doubt, was the opposite. A blessed race had made for itself this retreat beloved of birds, flowers, of pure air and sunlight.

"These," my guide informed me, "are the ancient inhabitants of the mountain dominating the city and upon which we now stand. They have lived here for a long time, with their simple customs, kindly and just, preserving the natural virtues of the world's earliest days. The people round about honored them and modeled themselves upon them."

Following my guide I descended from the point where I was to one of those tall dwellings, the joined roofs of which presented such a strange appearance. It seemed to me as though my feet were sinking into successive layers of buildings of various ages. These ghostly edifices continually kept on uncovering others in which the style of each individual century was visible. To me they looked like the excavations of old cities, except that they were airy, animated, and crossed with thousands of rays of light. Finally I found myself in a vast hall where I saw an old man working at a table at something I could not recognize. The moment I crossed the threshold a man, dressed in white, whose face I was not able to see clearly, threatened me with a weapon he held in his hand: but my guide signed to him to go away. It appeared as though they had wished to stop me from penetrating the mysteries of these retreats. Without asking my guide anything, I intuitively understood that these heights — and depths also — were the sanctuary of the primitive inhabitants of the mountain. Continually stemming the advancing waves of new races, they lived there, with their simple customs, loving and just, clever, brave, and inventive, quietly conquering the blind masses who had so many times encroached on their heritage. They were, in fact, neither corrupted, nor destroyed, nor enslaved! They were pure although they had conquered ignorance, and they had preserved in prosperity the virtues of poverty! A child was on the floor playing with crystals, shells and engraved stones, no doubt turning its lesson into a game. An elderly, but still beautiful, woman was busying herself with her household duties. Then several young people came in noisily, as though returning from work. I was amazed to see them all dressed in white; but it seemed that this was an optical illusion on my part; to make this clear to me my guide began to draw their costumes for me and give them bright colors, making me understand what they were like in reality. The whiteness that surprised me came, perhaps, from some especial brilliancy, from a trick of light in which the ordinary hues of the prism became confused.

I left the room and found myself on a terrace laid out as a garden. Here young girls and little children were walking about and playing. Their clothes seemed to me to be white like the others, but they were trimmed with pink embroidery. These young people were so beautiful, their features so graceful, and the light of their souls shone so vividly from their delicate forms, that they all inspired a sort of love without preference and devoid of all desire, an epitome of all the intoxications of the vague passions of youth.

I cannot communicate the feelings I had among these charming creatures who, although strangers, were very dear to me. They were like a primitive, heavenly family whose smiling eyes sought mine in soft compassion. I began to shed scalding tears as if at the memory of some lost paradise. I felt bitterly that I was only a wayfarer in this strange land that I loved, and I trembled at the thought that I had to return to life. In vain the girls and children pressed round me to try to detain me. Already their enchanting forms were melting in a misty confusion; their lovely faces faded, their clear-cut features and sparkling eyes vanished into a shadow where still shone the last gleam of a smile…

Such was that vision, or such at least the main details I can remember. The cataleptic state in which I had been for some days was explained away to me in scientific terms, and the remarks of those who had seen me then irritated me when I realized that they attributed to mental aberration my actions and words which coincided with the various phases of what were for me a series of logical events. But I felt a greater affection than ever for those of my friends who, from kindness or patience, or because of a set of ideas similar to mine, made me give long accounts of the things I had seen in my mind. With tears in his eyes, one of them said to me:

"Is it not true there is a God?"

"Yes!" I answered enthusiastically.

And we embraced each other, like two brothers of that mystic country I had half-seen. What happiness I found at first in that belief! For thus the eternal doubt about the immortality of the soul, which troubles the greatest minds, had been solved for me. No more death, no more sadness, no more cares. My loved ones, relatives, and friends, had given convincing proof of their eternal existence, and I was only separated from them by the hours of the day. I waited for the hours of the night with a gentle melancholy.

VI

Another dream of mine confirmed me in this belief. I suddenly found myself in a room which formed part of my grandfather's house, only it seemed to have grown larger. The old furniture glowed with a miraculous polish, the carpets and curtains were as if new again, daylight three times more brilliant than natural day came in through the windows and the door, and in the air there was a freshness and perfume like the first warm morning of spring. Three women were working in the room and, without exactly resembling them, they stood for relatives and friends of my youth. Each seemed to have the features of several of them. Their facial contours changed like the flames of a lamp, and all the time something of one was passing to the other. Their smiles, the color of their eyes and hair, their figures and familiar gestures, all these were exchanged as if they had lived the same life, and each was made up of all three, like those figures painters take from a number of models in order to achieve a perfect beauty.

The eldest spoke to me in a vibrant, melodious voice which I recognized as having heard in my childhood, and whatever it was she said struck me as being profoundly true. But she drew my attention to myself and I saw I was wearing a little old-fashioned brown suit, entirely made of needlework threads as fine as a spider's web. It was elegant, graceful, and gently perfumed. I felt quite rejuvenated and most spruce in this garment which their fairy fingers had made, and I blushingly thanked them as if I had been a small boy in the presence of beautiful grown-up ladies. At that moment one of them got up and went towards the garden.

It is a well-known fact that no one ever sees the sun in a dream, although one is often aware of some far brighter light. Material objects and human bodies are illumined through their own agencies. Now I was in a little park through which ran long vine arbors loaded with heavy clusters of black and white grapes; and as the lady, guiding me, passed beneath these arbors, the shadows of the intertwined trelliswork changed her figure and her clothes. At last we came out from these bowers of grapes to an open space. Traces of the old paths which had once divided it crosswise were just visible. For some years the plants had been neglected and the sparse patches of clematis, hops and honeysuckle, of jasmine ivy, and creepers, had stretched their long clinging tendrils between the sturdy growths of the trees. Branches of fruit were bowed to the ground and a few garden flowers, in a state of wildness now, bloomed among the weeds.

At distant intervals were clumps of poplars, acacias and pine trees, and in the midst of these were glimpses of statues blackened by time. I saw before me a heap of rocks covered with ivy, from which gushed a spring of fresh water whose splashes echoed melodiously over a pool of still water, half-hidden by huge water lilies.

The lady I was following stretched her slender figure in a movement that made the folds of her dress of shot taffeta shimmer, and gracefully she slid her bare arm about the long stem of a hollyhock. Then, in a clear shaft of light, she began to grow in such a way that gradually the whole garden blended with her own form and the flowerbeds and trees became the patterns and flounces of her clothes, while her face and arms imprinted their contours on the rosy clouds in the sky. I lost her thus as she became transfigured, for she seemed to vanish in her own immensity.

"Don't leave me!" I cried. "For with you Nature itself dies."

With these words I struggled painfully through the brambles trying to grasp the vast shadow that eluded me. I threw myself on a fragment of ruined wall, at the foot of which lay the marble bust of a woman. I lifted it up and felt convinced it was of *her*... I recognized the beloved features and as I stared around me I saw that the garden had become a graveyard, and I heard voices crying: "The universe is in darkness."

VII

This dream, which began so happily, perplexed me deeply, for I did not discover what it meant until much later. Aurélia was dead.

At first I only heard that she was ill. Owing to my state of mind I only felt a vague unhappiness mixed with hope. I believed that I myself had only a short while longer to live, and I was now assured of the existence of a world in which hearts in love meet again. Besides, she belonged to me much more in her death than in her life... A selfish enough thought for which my reason later paid with bitter remorse.

I did not like abusing a presentiment, however. Chance does strange things. But at that time I was still obsessed by a memory of our too rapid union. I had given her a ring of antique workmanship whose stone was a heart-shaped opal. As this ring was too big for her finger, I had conceived the fatal idea of having it cut down; I only realized my mistake when I heard the noise of the saw. I seemed to see blood flowing...[5]

Medical treatment had restored me to health without having yet brought my mind back to the regular functioning of human reason. The house I was in was on a hill and had a large garden full of valuable trees. The pure air of the slopes on which it stood, the first breath of spring, the pleasure of a sympathetic society, all brought me long days of calm.

I was enchanted by the vivid colors of the early sycamore leaves, like the crests of cock pheasants. From morning to evening one could gaze over the plain to charming horizons, the graduated hues of which delighted my imag-ination. I peopled the hills and clouds with heavenly figures whose shapes I seemed to see distinctly. I wanted to fix my favorite thoughts more clearly, and with some charcoal and a few bits of brick that I collected I had soon covered the walls with a set of frescoes recording my impressions. One face dominated the rest — that of Aurélia, painted in the shape of a divinity, as she had appeared to me in my dream. Beneath her feet a wheel was turning and the gods processed behind her. I succeeded in coloring this group by crushing out the juice from plants and flowers. How many times have I dreamed in front of that dear idol! I did more, I tried to shape the body of my beloved in clay. Every morning I had to begin again, for the lunatics, jealous of my happiness, took pleasure in destroying its image.

I was given paper, and for a long time I set about producing, by means of verses and inscriptions in every known language and a thousand forms and stories, a sort of world history mingled with memories of my studies and fragments of dreams made more plausible by my obsession (which was itself prolonged by them). I did not confine myself to the modern traditions of creation. My thoughts went further. As if in memory I caught a glimpse of the first covenant made, by means of talismans, by the genii of old. I tried to put together again the stones of the *sacred table* and to represent around it the first seven *Elohim* who shared the world.

This system of history, borrowed from Oriental tradition, began with the peaceful agreement of the powers of nature who formed and organized the universe. The night before I worked, I imagined myself transported to a dark planet where the first germs of creation were struggling. From the bosom of the still-soft clay, gigantic palm trees towered high, poisonous spurge and acanthus writhed around cactus plants: the arid shapes of rocks stuck out like skeletons from this rough sketch of creation, and hideous reptiles snaked, stretched, and coiled in the middle of the inextricable network of wild vegetation. Only the pale light of the stars lit the bluing perspectives of this strange horizon; yet, as the work of creation proceeded, a brighter star began to draw from it the germs of its own future brilliance.

VIII

Then the monsters changed shape. They cast off their first skins and raised themselves up more powerfully on their enormous paws. The great mass of their bodies crushed the branches and vegetation, and in this chaos of nature they engaged in struggles in which I myself was part, for I had a body as strange as theirs. Suddenly a singular harmony echoed through our solitudes and it seemed as if the confused cries, roarings and hissings of these primitive beings now took on this celestial melody. Infinite variations followed, the planet grew gradually lighter, heavenly shapes appeared among the shrubs and in the depths of the groves and, thus mastered, all the monsters I had seen shed their weird shapes and became men and women; others, in their reincarnations, assumed the bodies of wild animals, fishes and birds.

Who had performed this miracle? A radiant goddess guided the speedy evolution of man through these new *metamorphoses.*[6] A distinct race was established. Beginning with the birds, it comprised also animals, fishes and reptiles. There were Divas, Peris, undines and salamanders. Whenever one of the creatures died, it was immediately born again in a more beautiful form and sang the glory of the gods. But one of the Elohim conceived the idea of creating a fifth race composed of earthly elements and to be called *Afrites*. This was the signal for a complete revolution among the Spirits who did not wish to recognize these new lords of the world. I do not know for how many thousands of years these battles raged drenching the earth in blood. Finally, three of the Elohim, together with the spirits of their race, were relegated to the south of the world where they founded vast kingdoms. They had taken with them the secrets of the heavenly *cabala* which link the worlds, and they had gathered strength from the adoration of certain stars with which they were always in correspondence. These necromancers, exiled to the ends of the earth, had agreed to transmit their power to one another. Surrounded by women and slaves, each of their sovereigns was assured of being born again in the form of one of his children. Their life lasted a thousand years. When they were about to die, powerful cabalists shut them up in well-guarded tombs where they were fed elixirs and life-giving substances. They preserved the semblance of life for a long time. Then, as the chrysalis spins its cocoon, they fell asleep for forty days to be born again as a little child which was later called to the kingdom.

The vivifying forces of the world, however, were exhausted in feeding these families, whose blood went continually to fertilize fresh offsprings. In vast subterranean chambers, hollowed in hypogea and pyramids, they had collected all the treasures of past races and certain talismans which protected them against the anger of the gods.

These strange mysteries took place in central Africa, beyond the Mountains of the Moon and ancient Ethiopia: for a long time I groaned there in captivity together with a whole section of the human race. The groves I had once seen so green bore only pale flowers now and faded foliage: an inexorable sun consumed these regions, and the weak children of the eternal dynasties seemed crushed beneath the weight of life. This impressive and monotonous grandeur, ruled by custom and priestly ritual, was a burden on all, yet no one dared escape it. The old men languished under the weight of their crowns and imperial ornaments, among the doctors and priests whose knowledge guaranteed their immortality. As for the masses, they were fixed forever in a caste system, and could be certain of neither life nor liberty. At the feet of trees smitten with death or sterility, at the mouths of dried-up springs, children withered and pale girls weakened away on the scorched grasses. The splendor of the royal rooms, the majesty of the porticos, the brilliance of robes and ornaments, all these were poor consolations for the eternal dreariness of these solitudes.

Soon illness ravaged the people, plants and animals died, and the immortals themselves wasted away under their pompous costumes. A scourge, more terrible than any before, came suddenly to rejuvenate and save the world. Orion let loose cataracts of water in the heavens. Earth, overweighted by ice at its opposite pole, half-turned on its axis, and the oceans overflowed their banks and poured over the plains of Africa and Asia. The flood saturated the sands, filled the tombs and pyramids, while for forty days a mysterious ark floated on the waters, bearing the hope of a new creation.

Three of the Elohim had taken refuge on the peak of the highest mountain in Africa. They began fighting. Here my memory grows vague, and I do not know the result of their battle. But I can still see a woman standing on a peak lapped by the waters they abandoned, crying out with disheveled hair and struggling against death. Her pitiful cries rose above the noise of the waters... Was she saved? I do not know. Her brothers, the gods, had condemned her; but over her shone the Evening Star throwing its flaming rays upon her forehead.

The interrupted hymn of heaven and earth resounded again in harmony to hallow the agreement of the new races. Noah and his sons toiled painfully under the rays of a new sun and the sorcerers, crouched in their underworld, still kept their treasures there and reveled in the silence and the darkness. Sometimes they issued timidly out of their fastnesses and came to frighten the living or spread the disastrous lessons of their knowledges among the wicked.

Such were the memories I retraced by a sort of vague intuition of the past: I shuddered as I reproduced the hideous characteristics of those accursed races. Everywhere the suffering image of the eternal Mother was dying, weeping, or languishing. All through remote Asiatic and African civilizations a bloody scene of orgy and carnage was constantly renewed, reproduced by the same spirits under different forms.

The last one took place at Granada, where the sacred talisman fell before the hostile blows of Christians and Moors. How many more years yet has the world still to suffer, for the vengeance of those eternal enemies must inevitably be renewed under other skies! They are the severed sections of the serpent that encircles the Earth... separated by steel, they join together again in a hideous embrace cemented by human blood.

IX

Such were the visions which filed, one by one, before my eyes. Gradually calm came back to me and I left the house which had been a paradise for me. A long while later fateful circumstances brought about a relapse which renewed this interrupted series of strange dreams.

I was walking in the country, preoccupied with some work connected with religious ideas. I passed in front of a house and heard a bird repeating some words it had been taught. Yet this muddled prattling seemed to me to have some sense. It reminded me of the bird in the vision I have recounted above, and I shuddered with a foreboding of evil.

A few steps further on I met a friend whom I had not seen for a long time, and who lived in a house nearby. He wanted to show me his estate and in the course of doing so he made me climb a raised terrace with him, from which could be seen a wide view. It was sunset. As we descended the steps of a rustic stair I stumbled and struck my chest against the angle of a piece of garden furniture. I had just enough strength left to get up and dash into the middle of the garden, thinking I had received a death blow and wanting, before I died, to cast a last glance at the setting sun. Through all the regrets that such a moment brings, I felt happy to be dying this way, at this hour, surrounded by the trees, trellises and autumn flowers. It was, however, no more than a swoon and I soon recovered sufficiently to return home and go to bed. I had an attack of fever. When I thought of the spot where I had fallen, I remembered that the view I had so admired overlooked a cemetery, the very one that housed Aurélia's grave. I had not really thought of it until then; otherwise I might have attributed my fall to the impression which the sight of it had made on me. That very circumstance gave me the idea of a more certain fatality and I regretted the more that death had not reunited me to her. Then, as I thought it over, I told myself that I was unworthy of it. I reviewed with bitterness the life I had led since her death and reproached myself, not with having forgotten her, which had not been the case, but with having outraged her memory in facile love affairs. Then I thought I would appeal to sleep; but *her* image, which had so often appeared to me, no longer returned to my dreams. At first my impressions were confused, and mixed with scenes of bloodshed. It seemed to me that a whole fatal race had been let loose in that ideal world I had previously seen, and of which she was the queen. The same Spirit who had threatened me when I entered the dwelling of those pure families who lived in the *Mysterious City* passed before me, no longer in the white robes he had worn then, together with the rest of his race, but dressed like an Oriental prince. I rushed towards him, threateningly, but he turned calmly and — to my terror and fury — it was my own face, my whole form magnified and idealized... Then I remembered the man who had been arrested on the same night as myself and whom, as I thought, the guard had released under my name when my two friends came to fetch me. In his hand he held some weapon the shape of which I could not properly see, and one of those with him said: "That was what he struck him with."

I find it impossible to explain how in my own mind earthly events could coincide with those of the supernatural world; it is easier to *feel* than to express clearly.* But what was this Spirit who was me and yet outside me? Was it the *Double* of the old legends, or that mystical brother Oriental people call *ar-ruh?*[7] Had I not once been struck by the story of the knight who had fought a whole night long in a forest against an unknown enemy who was himself? However that may be, I do not think that human imagination has invented anything which is not true either in this world or in others, and I

---

*To me this referred to the blow I received in my fall.

could not doubt what I had so clearly *seen* myself.

I had a terrible idea. Every man has a double, I said to myself. "I feel two men in myself," a Father of the Church once wrote.[8] The concurrence of two souls has infused this double seed in man's body, which shows similar halves in every organ of its structure. In everyone is a spectator and an actor, one who speaks and one who answers. The Orientals have seen two enemies in that, the good and evil genius of a man.

Am I the good or the evil? I asked myself. In any case my *other* is hostile to me... Who knows if there is not under certain circumstances or at a certain age in life a separation of these two spirits? They are both attached to the same body by material affinity, perhaps one is destined to honor and happiness, the other to annihilation and eternal suffering?

Suddenly a terrible flash of light pierced these obscurities... Aurélia was no longer mine... I thought I heard talk of a ceremony that was taking place somewhere else, and the preparations for a mystical marriage — my own — in which the *other* was to profit by the mistakes of my friends and of Aurélia herself. The dearest friends who came to see me and console me appeared uncertain, that is, the two halves of their souls were separated in relation to me, one side affectionate and confiding, the other full of death as far as I was concerned. In everything that these people said to me there was a double meaning even though they themselves were not aware of it since they were not living *in the spirit,* as I was. For an instant even this idea seemed comic when I thought of Amphitryon and Sosia. But what if this grotesque symbol were something else, what if it were, as in other old fables, the fatal truth under the mask of folly? Well, I told myself, I must fight against this spirit of destiny, fight even against God himself with the weapons of tradition and science. Whatever he may do in the shadow and the night, I exist — and to conquer him I have all the time left me for life on this earth.

X

How can I describe the strange despair to which these ideas gradually reduced me? An evil genius had my place in the soul world. Aurélia would take him for me, and the wretched spirit that animated my body, weakened, disdained, and unrecognized by her, saw itself eternally destined to despair or annihilation. I used all my will power to penetrate further that mystery whose veils I had partly lifted. At times my dreams mocked my efforts and only brought me grimacing and fugitive faces. Here I can give only a rather odd idea of the result of this strife in my spirit. I felt I was sliding on a tightrope of infinite length. Earth, streaked with colored veins of molten metals, as I had already seen it, gradually grew brighter with the expansion of its central fire, whose whiteness was tinged with the pink glow that colored the walls of the inner globe. From time to time I was amazed to find large pools of water hanging in the air like clouds, and yet of such density that one could pick flakes off them. But it was clear that this was a different kind of liquid from earthly water, and that it was no doubt the evaporation of what constituted oceans and rivers in the spirit world.

I came to a huge, hilly shore, covered with a kind of reed, of a greenish color but yellowed at the tips as if partially shrivelled by the heat of the sun — yet I did not see the sun any more than on any other occasion. A castle dominated the hillside which I now began to climb. On the further slope of this an immense city lay stretched out. While I was crossing the hill, night had fallen and I saw lights in the houses and streets. On my way down I found myself in a market where they were selling fruit and vegetables like those in the South of France.

I went down by a dark flight of steps and found myself in the streets. The opening of a casino was being advertised and the details of its arrangements were being announced in posters. The typographical borders of these posters were composed of garlands of flowers so well drawn and colored they seemed real. Part of the building was still under construction. I went into a workshop where I saw workmen modeling in clay an enormous animal, the shape of a llama but apparently to be armed with great wings. This beast was as though impregnated with a jet of fire which gradually gave it life and made it writhe, pierced by a myriad purple threads forming veins and arteries, and fertilizing, so to speak, the inert matter which became covered instantaneously with a vegetation of fibrous appendages, fins, and tufts of wool. I stopped to look at this masterpiece in which, it seemed, the secrets of divine creation had been surprised.

"We have here," I was told, "the primitive fire which animated the first living creatures... At one time it used to reach the earth's surface, but the springs have dried up now."

I saw also jewelers' work in which two metals, unknown on earth, were used: one was red, and seemed to correspond to cinnabar, and the other was azure blue. The ornaments were neither hammered nor cut, but they took their shape and color and began to spread out like metallic plants produced by certain chemical reactions.

"Do you not create men, too?" I asked one of the workmen.

But he answered: "Men come from above and not from below. How could we possibly create ourselves? All we do here is to formulate, through successive advances of our industries, a more subtle matter than the one that forms the earth's crust. These flowers which seem natural to you, this animal which will appear to live, these will be merely the products of art, raised to the highest point of our knowledge, and everyone will look on them as such."

These were approximately the words which were either spoken to me or whose meaning I thought I could feel. I began to wander through the rooms of the casino where I saw a dense crowd, among whom I recognized several people I knew, some of them alive and some who had died at various times in the past. The former seemed not to see me, while the others answered me without appearing to know me. I now came to the largest room. It was completely hung with flame-colored velvet richly decorated with gold braid. In the center of this room was a couch in the shape of a throne. Some of the people passing by sat down on it to test its springiness; but as the preparations were not yet completed, they went into other rooms. There was some talk of a marriage and of the bridegroom who, they said, was to come and announce the beginnings of the festivities. Immediately a mad rage seized me. I imagined that the man they were waiting for was my *double,* and that he was going to marry Aurélia. I made a row, the gathering was thrown into consternation, and I began to speak violently, explaining my wrongs and calling on those who knew me for help. One old man said to me: "But you can't behave like this, you're frightening everyone."

I shouted out: "I know he has struck me once with his weapon, but I am not afraid and await him, knowing the sign with which to defeat him."

At that moment there appeared one of the workmen from the workshop I had visited. He was holding a long bar at the tip of which was a red-hot ball. I wanted to fling myself upon him, but the ball which he held out before him seemed to be continually threatening my head. Everyone around me seemed to be jeering at my impotence... I stepped back to the throne then, my soul filled with unutterable pride, and raised my arm to make a sign which to me appeared to have magical power. A woman's cry, vibrant and clear, and filled with excruciating agony, woke me with a start. The syllables of the unknown word I had been about to utter died on my lips... I threw myself on the floor and began praying fervently, weeping warm tears. But whose was the voice which had rung with such suffering through the night?

It was not part of my dream; it was the voice of a living person, and yet for me it was the voice and tone of Aurélia...

I opened my window. All was quiet and the cry was not repeated. I enquired outside. No one had heard anything. Yet I was still positive that the cry had been real and that the air of the real world had rung with it... Doubtless they would tell me that through a coincidence a woman in pain had cried out somewhere near the house at just that second. But in my belief terrestrial events were linked up with those of the invisible world. It is one of those strange relationships which I do not understand myself, and which it is easier to hint at than define...

What had I done? I had disturbed the harmony of the magic universe, from which my soul drew the certainty of immortal existence. Perhaps I was cursed for having offended divine law by wishing to penetrate a terrible mystery. I could only expect anger and scorn! The furious shadows fled shrieking, describing fatal circles in the air, like birds before the approach of a storm.

P A R T   T W O

Eurydice! Eurydice![9]

I

Lost once more!

All is finished, it is all over. Now I must die and die without hope. What then is death? Nothingness?... Would to God it were! But God himself cannot make death a nothingness.

Why do I think of *him* for the first time for so long? The system of destiny created in my mind admitted no such single sovereignty... or rather that royalty was merged in the sum of all beings... it was the god of Lucretius, powerless and forlorn in his own immensity.

She, however, believed in God and one day I surprised the name of Jesus on her lips. It slipped from them so softly that I wept. Dear God, those tears, those tears... they have been dry for so long. Give back those tears to me, O God.

When the soul drifts uncertainly between life and the dream, between the mind's disorder and the return to cool reflection, it is in religious thought that we should seek consolation; such I have never found in a philosophy which only gives us egotistical maxims or, at most, those twin tenets, empty experience and bitter doubt: it struggles against moral anguish by annihilating sensibility; like surgery, it can only cut out the suffering organ. But for us, born in days of revolutions and storms, when every belief was broken, brought up at best in a vague tradition satisfied by a few external observances, the indifferent adhesion to which is perhaps worse than impiety and heresy — for us it is very difficult, when we feel the need of it, to resurrect that mystic edifice already built in their ready hearts by the innocent and the simple. "The tree of knowledge is not the tree of life!" And yet, can we cast out of our spirits all the good or evil poured into them by so many learned generations? Ignorance cannot be learned.

I hope better of the goodness of God. Perhaps we are approaching the predicted time when science, having completed its cycle of analysis and synthesis, of belief and negation, will be able to purify itself and raise up the marvelous city of the future out of the confused ruins... We must not hold human reason so cheap as to believe it gains by complete self-humiliation, for that would be to impeach its divine origin... God will no doubt appreciate purity of intention; and what father would like to see his son give up all reason and pride in front of him? The apostle who had to touch to believe was not cursed for his doubt!

★

What have I been writing? Blasphemies. Christian humility does not speak in that way. Such thoughts are far from softening the soul. On their foreheads they bear the proud glitter of Satan's crown... A pact with God himself?... O science! O vanity!

★

I had got together several books on the cabala. I sank myself in study of these and succeeded in persuading myself that everything accumulated there by the human spirit over the centuries was true. The conviction I had formed of the existence of the exterior world coincided so well with my reading that I could no longer doubt the revelations of the past. The dogmas and rituals of various religions seemed to tally with it to such a degree that each one had in it a certain portion of those secrets, which constituted its means of expansion and defense. These powers could weaken, lessen, and disappear altogether, and this led to the invasion of certain races by others — none, however, could conquer or be conquered except by the Spirit.

"Yet," I told myself, "it is certain that human errors are intermingled in these sciences. The magic alphabet, the mysterious hieroglyphs have only come down to us incomplete and falsified, either by time or by men who have an interest in our remaining ignorant. Let us rediscover the lost letter, the effaced sign, let us recompose the dissonant scale, and we shall gain power in the world of the spirits."

Thus I thought I saw correspondences between the real world and the spirit world. The earth, its inhabitants and their history, were the theater in which we carried out the physical actions which prepared the existence and position of the immortal beings attached to its destiny. Without discussing the impenetrable mystery of the eternity of worlds, my thoughts went back to that time when the sun, like the flower that represents it and follows with bowed head its course in the skies, sowed on earth the fruitful seeds of plants and animals. It was nothing but this very ball of fire which being a composite of souls, instinctively formed the common dwelling place. The spirit of the Godhead, reproduced and, so to speak, reflected on earth, became the common type of human soul of which each was at once both God and man. Such were the Elohim.

★

When we feel unhappy we think of the unhappiness of others. I had neglected to call on one of my best friends who I had heard was ill.[10] As I went to the place where he was being treated, I reproached myself sharply for this omission. I was all the more miserable when my friend told me that he had been worse the night before. I went into a whitewashed hospital ward. The sun traced cheerful triangular patterns on the walls and played on a vase of flowers which a nun had just arranged on the sick man's table. It was almost the cell of an Italian anchorite. His wasted face, the ivory-yellow of his skin, accentuated by the blackness of his beard and his hair, his eyes glittering with the last of the fever, perhaps also something in the arrangement of the hooded cloak flung over his shoulders, all this made him a somewhat different person from the man I had known. He was no longer the happy comrade of my work and play. There was something of the apostle about him. He described to me how, at the worst stage in his sufferings, he had been seized by a final delirium that had seemed to him the supreme moment. Immediately his pain had ceased as if by a miracle. It is impossible to convey what he then told me — a blissful dream in the vaguest spaces of infinity, a conversation with a being at once different from, and bound to, himself, whom he asked where God was, as he imagined himself dead. "But God is everywhere," his spirit answered. "He is in you yourself and in us all. He judges you, listens to you, advises you: you and *I* think and dream together, we have never left one another, and we are eternal!"

I cannot quote any more of this conversation which I perhaps heard or understood badly. I only know that the impression it left on me was a deep one. I dare not attribute to my friend conclusions that perhaps I myself drew falsely from his words. I do not even know if the resultant feeling is compatible with Christianity or not.

"God is with him!" I exclaimed to myself. "But he is no longer with me. Oh, misery, I have driven him from me, I have threatened him, I have cursed him! It was indeed he, the mystic brother, who drifted further and further from my soul and warned me in vain. The Beloved Bridegroom, King of Glory, it is he who has judged and condemned me, and taken to his own heaven the woman he gave me and of whom I am now unworthy forever!"

II

I cannot describe the dejection into which these ideas threw me.

"I understand," I said to myself, "I have preferred creature to Creator; I have deified my love and adored with pagan ritual her whose last sigh was consecrated to Christ. But if his religion is sincere, God may yet forgive me. He may give me her back if I humble myself before him; perhaps his spirit will return to me."

Thinking this, I wandered aimlessly through the streets. A funeral procession crossed my path, going to the cemetery where she was buried. I felt impelled to join the procession and go there.

"I do not know," I said to myself, "who this dead person is they are taking to burial; but I know now that the dead see and hear us; perhaps this

person will be glad of a brother in sorrow, sadder than any of those follow-
ing now."

This idea made me shed tears and no doubt they thought I was one of
the deceased's best friends. O blessed tears! Your sweetness had been denied
to me for so long!... My head grew clearer and a ray of hope led me on. I
felt the power of prayer and took a delirious enjoyment in it.

I did not find out the name of the person whose coffin I had followed.
The cemetery I went into was sacred to me for several reasons. Three of my
mother's family had been buried there; but I could not go and pray on their
graves for they had been taken away years ago to that distant country, their
original home. For some time I looked for Aurélia's tomb but could not find
it. The cemetery had been rearranged — perhaps also my memory had
strayed... It seemed to me that this accident, this forgetfulness, added more
to my damnation. I dared not mention to the officials the name of a dead
woman over whom I had no religious rights... Then I remembered that in
my room I had the exact plan of where her tomb was, and I ran back there,
my heart pounding, my head distracted. I have already admitted how I sur-
rounded my love with weird superstitions. In a little casket that had once
belonged to *her* I kept her last letter. Dare I confess that I had made out of
this casket a kind of reliquary which had brought back to me long travels in
which the thought of her had followed me — a rose gathered in the gardens
of Schoubrah, a strip of mummy-cloth brought back from Egypt, some laurel
leaves from the river at Beirut, two little gilded crystals, mosaics from Saint
Sophia, a rosary bead, and other things I have forgotten... finally the paper
given me the day her grave was dug to enable me to find it again... I blushed.
My hands shook as I went through this crazy collection. I took the two

pieces of paper and just as I was about to set off once more for the ceme-
tery, I changed my mind.

"No," I told myself, "I am unworthy to kneel at a Christian woman's
tomb; let us not add another profanation to so many others."

Then, to pacify the storm raging through my brain, I went out some dis-
tance from Paris to a little town where I had once spent happy times in my
youth with some old relatives, since dead. I had often loved to go there to see
the sunset near their house. There was a walk shaded with lime trees which
brought back to me the memory of girls, relations, with whom I had grown
up. One of them...[11]

But could I ever have dreamed of comparing that vague childish love to
the one which consumed my youth? I saw the sun sinking over the valley full
of misty shadows; it vanished from sight, bathing the tips of the trees on the
edges of the little hills with a rosy glow. My heart filled with the deepest
sadness. I went and slept at an inn where I was known. The innkeeper spoke
to me of one of my old friends who lived in the town and who had blown
his brains out after some unlucky speculation... Sleep brought me dreadful
dreams. I have only a nebulous memory of them. I was in a room I did not
know and talking to someone from the outside world, perhaps the very friend
I have just mentioned. There was an extremely tall mirror behind us.
Happening to glance in it I thought I saw Aurélia. She seemed sad and pen-
sive, and suddenly, whether she came out of the mirror, or whether, passing
through the room, her reflection had appeared there for an instant, that sweet
beloved face was with me. She held out her hand, let a sad glance fall on me,
and said: "We shall meet again later... at your friend's house."

At once I thought of her marriage, the curse that kept us apart... and I said to myself: "Is it possible? Will she come back to me?"

And I asked with tears in my eyes: "Have you forgiven me?"

But everything had disappeared. I was in a deserted spot, a rough acclivity strewn with rocks, in the midst of forests. A house I seemed to know dominated this desolate landscape. I walked to and fro along tortuous paths. Tired of walking among rocks and briars I sometimes tried to find an easier way through openings of the wood.

"They are waiting for me over there!" I thought.

I heard a clock strike a certain hour... I said to myself: *"It's too late!"*

Voices answered me: *"She is lost!"*

Deep night surrounded me. The distant house glittered as though lit for a feast and as if full of guests who had arrived in good time.

"She is lost!" I cried out to myself. "And why?... I understand. She has made a last effort to save me; I missed the supreme moment when pardon was still possible. From highest heaven she could intercede for me with the Divine Spouse... and what does even my salvation matter? The abyss has claimed its prey! She is lost to me and lost to us all!..."

I seemed to see her in a flash of lightning, pale and dying, being borne away by dark horsemen...

The cry of pain and anger I uttered at that moment woke me up, panting.

"O God! O God! For her and her alone! Dear God, forgive me!" I cried, throwing myself on my knees.

It was day. As a result of an emotion it is difficult for me to explain, I immediately decided to destroy the two pieces of paper I had taken from the casket the night before — that last letter, alas, which, as I read it again, I wet with my tears, and the burial paper which bore the seal of the cemetery. "Find her tomb now!" I said to myself. "But I ought to have gone back there yesterday — and my fatal dream is but the reflection of a fatal day!"

III

The flames devoured these last relics of love and death which were attached to the most sensitive fibers of my heart. I went out into the country with my sorrows and belated remorse trying, by tiring myself out with walking, to deaden my thoughts and perhaps ensure a less distressing sleep for the following night. With my idea that dreams opened up to man intercourse with the spirit world, I hoped, I still had hope! Perhaps God would be content with this sacrifice. Here I paused; it is too presumptuous to pretend that my state of mind was brought about only by a memory of love. Let us say rather that I dressed up with this idea the keenest remorse at a life spent in foolish dissipation, a life in which evil had often triumphed, and whose errors I did not recognize until I felt the blows of misfortune. I no longer considered myself worthy to think of her, whom I had tormented in death having distressed her in life, and to whose sweet and sacred pity alone I owed a last glance of forgiveness.

The next night I only slept a few moments. A woman who had looked after me in my youth appeared to me in a dream and reproached me for a very serious fault I had once committed. I recognized her although she seemed much older than the last time I had seen her. This made me bitterly recall that I had neglected to visit her during her last moments. She seemed to say to me: "You did not weep for your old parents as much as you have for this woman. How then can you hope for forgiveness?" The dream grew confused. The faces of people I had known at various times passed rapidly in front of me. They filed past, becoming brighter, then fading, and falling back into the darkness like the beads of a broken rosary. Then I saw plastic images of antiquity vaguely take form before me, at first only in outline, and then more solidly; they seemed to represent symbols, whose meaning I grasped only with difficulty. Yet I think what it meant was: "All this was to teach you the secret of life and you have not understood it. Religions and legends, saints and poets, all concurred in explaining the fatal enigma, and you have inter- preted it wrongly... Now it is too late!"

I rose, terror-stricken, saying to myself: "This is my last day!" Ten years later the same idea that I have described in the first part of this narrative returned to me more definite and menacing. God had given me that time in which to repent, and I had not made use of it. After the apparition of the *Stone Guest*, I had sat down again to the feast!

IV

The emotion resulting from these visions and the reflections they brought during my solitude was so sad that I felt lost. Everything I had ever done in my life appeared under its most unfavorable aspect, and in the kind of scrutiny of conscience to which I subjected myself my memory served up to me the oldest facts with singular clarity. Some sense of false shame prevent- ed me from going to confess, perhaps the fear of involving myself in the dogmas and practices of a redoubtable religion, against certain points of which I had preserved philosophic prejudices. My early years were too impregnated with revolutionary ideas, my education had been too free, my life too rambling, for me to be able to accept easily a yoke which still, on many points, would offend my reason. I shuddered to think what kind of a Christian I should make, were it not that certain principles, borrowed from the freethinking of the past two centuries, combined with the study of comparative religion, had halted me on this declivity.

I never knew my mother, who had insisted on following my father on his campaigns, like the wives of the ancient Goths; she died of fever and exhaustion in a cold province of Germany, and my father himself had never been able to direct my early ideas that way. The part of the country where I was brought up was full of strange myths and odd superstitions. One of my uncles, who was the chief influence on my early education, occupied himself with Roman and Celtic antiques as a hobby. Sometimes he discovered, either on his land or nearby, effigies of gods and emperors, and his scholarly admiration made me regard these with deep respect, while I learnt their history from his lips. A certain statue of Mars in gilded bronze, an armed Pallas or Venus, a Neptune and Amphitrite sculpted over the village fountain, and, above all, the plump, jolly, bearded face of a Pan smiling at the entrance to a grotto festooned with aristolochia and ivy, these were the household gods who protected this retreat. I admit that they inspired me at that time with more veneration than did the poor Christian images in the church and the two battered saints in its portico, which some learned men asserted to be the Esus and Cernunnos of the Gauls. One day, feeling uncomfortable among all these different symbols, I asked my uncle what God was.

"God is the sun," he replied.

That was the private belief of an honest man who had lived all his life as a Christian, had passed through the Revolution, and who came from a district where many had the same idea of the Divinity. This did not prevent the women and children from going to church, and I owed to one of my aunts a certain amount of instruction that made me realize the beauty and grandeur of Christianity. After 1815, an Englishman who was in our part of the world made me learn the Sermon on the Mount and gave me a New Testament... I only mention these details to point out the causes for a certain irresolution which with me is frequently linked with a pronounced religious sentiment.

I want to explain how, after having been far from the true path for so long, I felt myself led back to it by the cherished memory of a dead person, and how my need to believe that she was still alive brought back into my mind a precise feeling for the various truths which I had not gathered firmly enough into my soul. Despair and suicide are the result of certain situations fatal for the man who has no faith in immortality, with all its sorrows and joys; I shall think I have done something good and useful by relating clearly the succession of ideas by means of which I recovered my peace of mind and a new strength with which to match the future misfortunes of life.

The successive visions of my sleep had reduced me to such despair that I could scarcely speak; the society of my friends gave me only a momentary distraction; my mind was wholly occupied by its illusions and refused to entertain the least different conception; I was unable to read and could not understand ten lines in a row. I said of the most beautiful things: "What do they matter? For me they do not exist."

One of my friends, called George,[12] undertook to overcome this despondency of mine. He took me out to various of the environs of Paris, and was content to do all the talking, while I only replied in a few disjointed phrases.

One day his expressive and quasi-monastic countenance seemed to give great import to the eloquence he was calling forth against the years of scepticism and political and social depression that had followed the July Revolution. I had been one of the young men of that period and I had tasted its ardors and bitternesses. An emotion took hold of me; I told myself that such lessons could not be given without the intention of Providence, and that no doubt a spirit was speaking through him... One day we were dining in an arbor in a little village near Paris. A woman came and sang close to our table, and something in her worn but sympathetic voice made me think of Aurélia's. I looked at her. Her very features were not unlike those I had loved. She was sent off, and I did not dare to detain her, but I said to myself: "Who knows? Perhaps *her spirit* is in that woman!" And I felt glad I had given her alms.

I said to myself: "I have misused my life, but if the dead forgive, then it is certainly on condition that we forever refrain from evil and repair all we have done wrong. Can that be?... From now on I will try to do no more evil and give back the equivalent of everything I owe."

I had recently wronged someone. It was only an act of negligence but I began by going and apologizing. The joy I obtained through act of reparation did me an immense amount of good; from then on I had a reason for living and acting, and I took a new interest in the world.

Difficulties arose. Inexplicable happenings seemed to collaborate to thwart my good resolution. My state of mind made the work I had promised impossible. As they thought me well now, people became more exacting, and, since I had given up telling lies, I found I was at a disadvantage in dealing with those who were not so hindered. The mass of reparations I had to make was crushing in proportion to my impotence. Political events worked indirectly, not only by worrying me but also by removing the means for my putting my affairs in order. The death of one of my friends completed these reasons for despondency. With sorrow I revisited his house, and saw the pictures he had so happily shown me a month before; I passed by his coffin at the moment when it was being nailed down. As he was my age and generation, I asked myself: "What would happen if I died suddenly like that?"

The following Sunday I got up in a fit of deep dejection. I went and saw my father whose maidservant was ill; he seemed in a bad temper. He insisted on going himself to get wood from the loft, and the only service I could render him was to hand him one log that he needed. I left in dismay. In the street I met a friend who wanted to take me along to dine with him in order to distract me a little. I refused his offer and, without having eaten anything, I made towards Montmartre. The cemetery was closed, which I considered an ill omen. A German poet[13] had given me a few pages of his to translate and had advanced me a sum for the work. I set off for his house to return him the money.

As I went through the Clichy gate, I saw a fight. I tried to separate the combatants but without success. At that moment a big workman crossed the very spot where the fight had been, carrying on his left shoulder a child in a hyacinth-colored dress.

I imagined that it was Saint Christopher carrying Christ and that I was condemned for not having had strength enough in the scene that had just taken place. From that moment on I wandered about in despair through the vague parts that divide the suburb from the city. It was too late to go on with my projected visit. So I went back through the streets towards the center of

Paris. Near the Rue de la Victoire I met a priest and in my distressed condition I wanted to confess to him. He told me that this was not his parish and that he was going out for an evening with a friend, but that, if I wanted to consult him on the following day at Notre-Dame, I had only to ask for Father Dubois.

In despair I went in tears to Notre-Dame de Lorette, where I threw myself at the foot of an altar to the Virgin, asking forgiveness for my sins. Something within me said: "Our Lady is dead, and your prayers are useless." I went and knelt at the very end of the choir and slipped from my finger a silver ring, whose stone was engraved with the three Arabic words: *Allah! Mohammed! Ali!* Immediately several candies were lit in the choir and a service began in which I tried to join in spirit. When the priest had got to the *Ave Maria,* he interrupted himself in the middle of the prayer and began again seven times, without my being able to remember the words that should have come next. The prayer over, the priest delivered a sermon which seemed to allude to me alone. When all the lights were extinguished, I got up and went out in the direction of the Champs-Élysées.

When I reached the Place de la Concorde, I thought of killing myself. Several times I started towards the Seine, but something stopped me from completing my plan. The stars shone in the sky. Suddenly it seemed to me that they were all extinguished like the candles I had seen in the church. I thought that the hour had arrived and that we had come to the end of the world predicted in the Apocalypse of Saint John. I thought I saw a black sun in an empty sky and a red ball of blood above the Tuileries. I said to myself: "The eternal night is beginning, and it will be terrible. What will happen when men find that there is no more sun?"

I returned by the Rue Saint-Honoré and pitied the belated country folk whom I met. When I came to the Louvre I walked as far as the square and there a strange sight greeted me. I saw several moons moving swiftly across the clouds, driven rapidly by the wind. I thought that the earth had left its orbit and was wandering through the firmament like a ship that had lost its masts, approaching or receding from the stars which grew alternately larger and smaller. I contemplated this chaos for two or three hours and then set out for Les Halles. The peasants were bringing in their produce, and I told myself: "How astonished they will be to see the night going on..." Yet here and there dogs were barking and cocks crowing.

Broken with weariness, I went home and threw myself on my bed. When I woke up, I was amazed to see the light. A kind of mysterious choir chanted in my ears. Childish voices were repeating in chorus: *"Christe! Christe! Christe!..."* I imagined they had collected a large number of children in the neighboring church (Notre-Dame-des-Victoires) to invoke Christ. "But Christ is no more!" I said to myself. "And they do not know it yet!"

The invocation lasted for about an hour. At last I got up and wandered under the galleries of the Palais-Royal. I told myself that probably the sun had retained enough strength to light the world for another three days, but that all the while it was using up its substance, and indeed I thought it looked cold and colorless. I stifled my hunger with a small cake in order to give myself strength to get as far as the German poet's house. When I got there I told him that it was all over and that we must be prepared for death. He called his wife who asked me: "What's the matter?"

"I don't know," I said. "I am lost."

She sent out for a cab, and a young girl took me to the hospital Dubois.

V

There my illness returned and took on various complications. At the end of a month I was better. For the next two months I resumed my wanderings around Paris. The longest journey I made was to visit the cathedral at Rheims. Gradually I began writing again and composed one of my best tales.[14] Yet I wrote with difficulty, nearly always in pencil on odd sheets, and according to the whim of my reverie or my walk. Correcting gave me endless trouble. A few days after I had published the work I was attacked by persistent insomnia. I went and walked about all night on the hill of Montmartre and there I watched the sun rise. I talked for hours with peasants and workmen. At other times I went to Les Halles. One night I dined in a café on the boulevard and amused myself by tossing gold and silver coins into the air. Then I went to the market and got into an argument with a total stranger whom I struck roughly; I do not know why nothing came of this. At a certain hour I heard the clock of Saint-Eustache strike and I began thinking of the battles between the Burgundians and the Armagnacs, and I imagined the ghosts of the warriors of that era around me. I picked a quarrel with a postman who wore on his chest a silver badge, and whom I accused of being the duke John of Burgundy. I tried to prevent him going into a bar. For some extraordinary and inexplicable reason his face filled with tears when he saw me threatening him with death. I felt softened and let him pass.

I went towards the Tuileries gardens, but they were shut. I then followed the quays and walked up to the Luxembourg. Then I returned to eat with one of my friends. After that I went to Saint-Eustache where I knelt piously at the altar of the Virgin and thought of my mother. The tears I shed relieved

my spirit and, on my way out of the church, I bought a silver ring. I then
went to see my father and as he was out I left him a bunch of marguerites. I
went to the Jardin des Plantes. There were a lot of people there and I stopped
for some time, watching the hippopotamus bathing in its pool.[15] Then I went
to the Natural History museum. The sight of the monsters there made me
think of the flood, and as I walked out a violent shower of rain came down
in the gardens.

I said to myself: "What bad luck! All these women and children will get
soaked!..." Then I thought: "But it's worse than that. A real flood is begin-
ning." The water rose in the neighboring streets; I ran down the Rue
Saint-Victor and, with the idea of halting what I believed to be the flooding
of the universe, I threw the ring I had bought at Saint-Eustache into the
deepest part. At that very moment the storm abated and the sun began to
shine.

Hope returned to my soul. I had arranged to meet my friend George at
four o'clock, and went to where he lived. Passing an antique shop, I bought
two velvet screens covered with hieroglyphic figures. It seemed to me that I
was consecrating the forgiveness of heaven. I got to George's house at the
right time and told him of my hopes. I was wet through and tired out. I
changed my clothes and lay down on his bed. During my sleep I had a mar-
velous vision. It seemed to me that the goddess appeared to me, saying: "I am
the same as Mary, the same as your mother, the same being also whom you
have always loved under every form. At each of your ordeals I have dropped
one of the masks with which I hide my features and soon you shall see me as
I really am." From the clouds behind her there appeared a lovely orchard, and
a soft, yet penetrating radiance illuminated this paradise. Although I only

heard her voice I felt myself plunged into a delicious intoxication. Soon afterwards I woke up and said to George: "Let's go out."

While we were crossing the Pont des Arts I explained the transmigration of souls to him, and said: "Tonight it seems to me that I have the soul of Napoleon in me, inspiring me and commanding me to do great things."[16]

In the Rue du Coq I bought a hat and, while George was waiting for the change from the gold piece I had thrown on the counter, I went on my way and came to the galleries of the Palais-Royal. There everyone seemed to be staring at me. A persistent idea had fixed itself in my mind that there were no more dead; I went through the Galerie de Foy saying: "I have committed a sin," and I could not find out what it was by consulting my memory which I believed to be that of Napoleon. "There is something here for which I have not paid!" With this idea in my mind I went into the Café de Foy and in one of the customers there I thought I could recognize old father Bertin of the Débats.[17] Then I crossed the gardens, somewhat interested in the little girls dancing in rings. I then left the galleries and made my way towards the Rue Saint-Honoré. I went into a shop to buy a cigar and, when I came out, the crowd was so dense I was nearly suffocated. I was extricated by three of my friends who got me into a café while one of them went in search of a cab. I was taken to the Hospice de la Charité.

During the night my delirium grew worse and more so in the early hours when I found I was tied down. I succeeded in freeing myself from the straitjacket and towards morning walked about the various wards. I had the idea that I had become like a god, possessed of powers of healing, so that I put my hands on some of the patients. Going up to a statue of the Virgin I took off its crown of artificial flowers in order to test the power in me. I walked in long strides, talking in an animated way of the ignorance of men who believed they could be cured by science alone, and seeing a bottle of ether on a table I drank it in one gulp. A hospital assistant, with a face I compared to an angel's, tried to stop me, but I was supported by neurotic strength and, just as I was about to overthrow him, I stopped and told him he did not understand my mission. Doctors came along then and I went on with my harangue on the impotence of their art. Then, though I had no shoes on, I went down the stairs and, coming to a garden, I went out and picked flowers there, strolling about on the grass.

One of my friends had returned to fetch me. So I left the garden and, while I was speaking to him, they thrust me into a straitjacket and made me get into a cab and I was taken away to an asylum outside Paris. As soon as I found myself among the insane, I realized that everything had been an illusion for me until then. However, the assurances that I attributed to the goddess Isis seemed to realize themselves by a series of trials to which I had to submit. So I accepted them with resignation.

The part of the house I was in looked out over a vast exercise ground, shaded by walnut trees. In one corner arose a little mound, where one of the inmates walked in a circle all day long. Others, like me, contented themselves with strolling on the platform or the path, which was bordered with grassy banks. On a wall to the west side were drawn figures, one of which represented the shape of the moon with geometrical eyes and mouth; over this face a kind of mask had been painted; the left wall was covered with various drawings in profile, one of which represented a sort of Japanese idol. Further on, a skull was carved in the plaster; on the opposite side, two stones had been sculpted into rather good gargoyles by one of the guests of the garden.

Two doors led down to cellars, which I imagined to be subterranean passages like those I had seen at the entrance to the Pyramids.

VI

At first I imagined that all the people collected in this garden had some influence over the stars, and that the man who was walking in an incessant circle was regulating the movement of the sun. One old man, brought there at certain hours of the day, who spent his time making knots and looking at his watch, seemed to me to be in charge of the task of verifying the passing of the hours. To myself I attributed an influence over the moon's course, and I believed it had been struck by thunder from the Almighty and that this had imprinted on its face the look of the mask I had noticed.

I gave a mystic significance to the conversations of the attendants and to those of my comrades. It seemed to me that these people were the representatives of every race in the world and that together we had to reorganize the courses of the stars and further develop the sidereal system. In my view there had been an error in the general combination of numbers and from that all humanity's ills arose. Further, I believed that the heavenly spirits had taken on human forms and were present at this kind of general congress, although they appeared to be occupied with ordinary affairs. My own role seemed to be to reestablish universal harmony by means of cabalistic arts and to seek a solution in summoning the occult powers of the various religions.

As well as the walk, there was another room for our use, whose windows with their perpendicular bars opened on a horizon of verdure. As I looked through these panes of glass at the lines of the outbuildings, I saw the facade and windows stand out like a thousand little pavilions ornamented with arabesques, topped with tracery work and spires, that reminded me of the imperial lodges along the shores of the Bosphorus. This naturally led my mind on to Oriental ideas. At about two o'clock I was put in a bath and I felt as if I were being attended by the Valkyries, the daughters of Odin, who wanted to raise me to immortality by gradually purging my body of its impurities.[18]

In the evening I walked about serenely in the moonlight and, when I looked up at the trees, their leaves seemed to me to curl up capriciously so as to form the figures of knights and ladies borne along on caparisoned steeds. For me they were the triumphant figures of our ancestors. That thought led me to think that there was a vast conspiracy between every living creature to reestablish the world in its original harmony, that communication took place by means of the magnetism of stars, that an unbroken chain around the earth linked the various intelligences devoted to this general communion, and that songs, dances, looks, magnetized from one to another, betrayed the same aspiration. For me the moon was the sanctuary of fraternal souls who had been relieved of their mortal bodies and who were working with greater freedom towards the regeneration of the universe.

Already the length of each day seemed to be increased by hours; so that, by rising at the hour fixed by the institution clocks, I was really only walking in the empire of shadows. My companions around me seemed to be asleep and to resemble specters of Tartarus, until the hour at which the sun rose for me. Then I greeted that luminary with a prayer, and my real life began.

From that moment on, when I felt sure that I was being subjected to the tests of a sacred initiation, an invincible strength entered into my soul. I imagined myself a hero living under the gaze of the gods; everything in Nature took on a new aspect, and secret voices, warning and exhorting me, came from plants, trees, animals, and the most lowly insects. The speech of my companions took mysterious turns, whose sense I alone could understand, and formless, inanimate objects lent themselves to the calculations of my mind; from combinations of pebbles, from shapes in corners, chinks or openings, from the outlines of leaves, colors, sounds, and smells, emanated for me hitherto unknown harmonies.

"How have I been able to live so long," I asked myself, "outside Nature without identifying myself with it? Everything lives, moves, everything corresponds; the magnetic rays, emanating either from myself or from others, cross the limitless chain of created things unimpeded; it is a transparent network which covers the world, and its slender threads communicate themselves by degrees to the planets and stars. Captive now upon earth, I commune with the chorus of the stars who share in my joys and sorrows."

Then I shuddered to think that even this mystery might be surprised. "If electricity," I told myself, "which is the magnetism of physical bodies, can be forced in a direction imposed on it by laws, that is all the more reason why hostile and tyrannical spirits may be able to enslave the intelligences of others, and make use of their divided strength for their own purposes of domination. Thus it was that the gods of old times were conquered and enslaved by new gods; and thus," I went on, consulting my memory of the ancient world, "that necromancers dominated entire peoples, whose succeeding generations became captive under their everlasting scepter. Ah misery! Death itself cannot free them! For we live again in our sons as we have lived in our fathers, and the relentless lore of our enemies can pick us out anywhere. The hour of our birth, the exact place on earth where we appear, the first movement, the name, the room, and all the consecrations and rituals imposed upon us, establish a lucky or unlucky series on which the whole of our future hangs. But while, by human reckoning, all this is already a terrible thought, realize what it implies when attached to the hidden formulas that set up the order of worlds. It has been rightly said that nothing is unimportant, nothing powerless in the universe; a single atom can dissolve everything, and save everything! What terror! There lies the eternal distinction between good and evil. Is my soul the indestructible molecule, the sphere inflated by a little air, which yet can find its place in nature, or is it that very void, a reflection of that nothingness which disappears in immensity? Or could it be that fateful particle destined to undergo, through all its transfigurations, the vengeance of powerful beings?" By this I was led to take account of my life and even of my previous existence. By proving to myself that I was good, I proved to myself that I must always have been good. "And if I have been evil," I said to myself, "will not my present life be sufficient expiation?" This thought reassured me, but did not free me from the fear of being forever classed among the unhappy. I felt myself thrust into cold water, and a colder water trickled down my forehead. I turned my thoughts to the eternal Isis, sacred mother and spouse; all my aspirations, all my prayers were mingled in that magic name, and I seemed to live again in her; sometimes she appeared to me in the guise of Venus of the ancients, sometimes as the Christian Virgin. Night made this dear vision clearer to me, and yet I asked myself: "What can she, conquered as she is and perhaps oppressed, do for her poor children?"

Pale and torn the crescent moon thinned each evening and soon perhaps we should never see her again in the sky! Yet it seemed that this celestial body was the refuge of all my sister souls, and I saw it peopled with plaintive shades, destined to be born again one day on earth...

My room lies at the end of a corridor, on one side of which live the insane, and on the other the asylum servants. It has only the privilege of one window, opening towards the courtyard, which is planted with trees and which in the daytime serves as an exercise ground. I love to gaze at a leafy walnut tree and two Chinese mulberries. Beyond, a busy street can be seen vaguely through the trelliswork, which is painted green. At sunset the horizon widens; it is like a hamlet with windows clothed in foliage or cluttered with bird cages and drying rags, from which occasionally appears the head of a young or old housewife, or the pink cheeks of a child. There are shouts, dancing, bursts of laughter; it is either gay or sad to hear, according to what hour it is and how it strikes one.

I found there all the remnants of my various fortunes, the confused remains of several sets of furniture scattered or sold over the past twenty years. It is a junk heap as bad as Doctor Faust's. A tripod table with eagles' heads, a console table supported on a winged sphinx, a seventeenth-century commode, an eighteenth-century bookcase, a bed of the same period with an oval-ceilinged baldaquin covered with scarlet damask (but this there was no room to erect), a rustic dresser laden with faïence and Sèvres porcelain, most of it somewhat damaged; a hookah brought back from Constantinople, a large alabaster cup, a crystal vase; some wood paneling from the destruction of an old house I had once lived in on the site of the Louvre, covered with mythological paintings done by friends who are today famous; two large canvases in the style of Prud'hon, representing the Muses of History and Comedy. For some days I amused myself by rearranging all these things, creating in this narrow attic an odd interior composed of palace and hovel, that aptly summarizes my wandering life. Over my bed I have hung my Arab clothes, my two carefully darned cashmere shawls, a pilgrim's flask, a game-bag. Above the bookshelves stretches an enormous map of Cairo; a bamboo bracket at the head of my bed supports a varnished Indian tray on which I can put my toilet articles. I was overjoyed to rediscover these humble relics of those years alternating in fortune and misery, to which the memories of my whole life are tied. They had put to one side only a little picture on copper, in the style of Correggio, showing *Venus and Love,* some pier glasses of nymphs and satyrs, and an arrow I had kept in memory of the bowmen of Valois to whom I used to belong in my youth; since the new laws had come in, the weapons had been sold. On the whole I found nearly everything I had previously possessed there. My books, an odd assortment of the knowledge of all ages, history, travels, religion, the cabala, astrology, enough to gladden the shades of Pico della Mirandola, the sage Meursius, and Nicholas of Cusa — the Tower of Babel in two hundred volumes — they had left me all that! They were enough to drive a wise man mad; let us try to ensure that there is enough to make a madman sane.

With what delight have I been able to file away in my drawers the mass of my notes and letters, correspondence both public and private, famous or obscure, as a chance meeting made them so, or a distant country I visited. In rolls, better wrapped than the others, I find Arabic letters, relics of Cairo and Stamboul. Oh joy! Oh mortal sorrow! These yellowed characters, these faded drafts, half-crumpled letters, these are the treasures of my only love… Let me read them again… Many of them are missing, others torn or scratched out; here is what I find:[19]

★   ★   ★

One night I was talking and singing in a kind of ecstasy. One of the warders came and fetched me from my cell, and made me go down to a room on the ground floor, where he shut me up. I went on with my dream and, although I was standing up, I imagined myself enclosed in a sort of Oriental pavilion. I felt all the corners and found it to be octagonal. A divan ran around the walls, which seemed to me to be of thick plate glass, beyond which I could see shining treasures, shawls, and tapestries. Across a street, a landscape was visible through the latticed door, and it seemed to me that I could distinguish the shapes of trees and rocks. I had already lived there in some other existence, and I thought I recognized the deep grottos of Ellora.[20] Gradually a bluish light penetrated the pavilion and brought out strange apparitions inside. I thought I was in the midst of some vast charnel house where the history of the universe was written in characters of blood.[21] Opposite me was painted the body of an enormous woman; but various parts of her had been sliced off, as if by a sword; on the other walls, other women of different races, whose bodies dominated me more and more, made a bloody jumble of limbs and heads, ranging from empresses and queens to the humblest peasants. It was the history of all crime, and I only had to keep my eyes on any one spot to see depicted there some tragic scene.

"There," I told myself, "is what has resulted from power bestowed on man. Man has little by little destroyed and cut up the eternal type of beauty into a thousand little pieces, so that his races are more and more losing strength and perfection..." And indeed, on a line of shadow creeping in through a chink in the door, I saw the descending generations of future races.

At last I was torn from these macabre reflections. The kind and compassionate face of my excellent doctor brought me back to the living world. He allowed me to witness something that interested me intensely. Among the patients was a young man, once a soldier in Africa, who had refused to take food for six weeks. By means of a long rubber tube introduced into one of his nostrils, they poured a quantity of semolina and chocolate into his stomach.

This sight made a deep impression on me. Until then I had been given up to the monotonous circle of my own sensations or moral sufferings, and here I met an unaccountable creature, patient and taciturn, seated like a sphinx at the last gates of existence. I began to love him because of his misfortune and abandonment, and I felt uplifted by this sympathy and pity. He seemed to me a sublime interpreter, placed between death and life, a confessor predestined to hear the soul's secrets which words dared not utter or could not succeed in expressing. It was the ear of God unsullied by another's thought. I spent hours in examining him mentally, my head bowed over his, and holding his hands. It seemed that a certain magnetism united our two spirits, and I was delighted the first time a word came from his mouth. No one would believe me, but I attributed this commencement of cure in him to my ardent will power. That night I had a marvelous dream, the first for a long time. I was in a tower, so deep in the earth and so high in the heavens, that all my life seemed to be passed in going up and down it. Already my strength was spent, and my courage failing, when a door in the side opened, a spirit appeared and said: "Come, brother!..."

I do not know why but I had the idea that he was called Saturninus. He possessed the features of the poor sick man, only transformed and intelligent. We were in a countryside lit with the glow of the stars and, as we stopped to look at them, the spirit figure placed his hand upon my forehead, as I had done, the night before, when I had endeavored to magnetize my companion. Immediately one of the stars I could see in the sky began to grow larger, and the divinity of my dreams appeared, smiling, in a somewhat Indian robe, as I had seen her before. She walked between us, and the meadows grew green, flowers and leaves sprang up from the earth in her footsteps... She said to me: "The ordeal you have undergone is coming to an end; these countless stairways which wore you out so going up and down are the bonds of old illusions that impeded your thoughts; now remember the day when you implored the Holy Virgin and, thinking her dead, were possessed of a frenzy of the mind. Your vow must be carried to her by a simple soul, one free from the ties of the earth. She is near you and that is why I myself have been permitted to come and encourage you."

This dream filled my spirit with joy and brought with it a wonderful awakening. Day was breaking. I wanted some material sign of the vision which had consoled me, and so I wrote these words on the wall: "This night you came to me."

Here, under the title of *Memorabilia,* I will put down the impressions of certain dreams which followed the one I have just described.

MEMORABILIA

★   ★   ★

The song of the shepherds has reechoed about a slender peak in Auvergne. *Poor Mary!* Queen of the heavens! It is you they are invoking so piously. The rustic melody has reached the ears of the Corybants. They emerge, singing also, from the secret caves where Love gave them shelter. Hosannah! Peace on earth and glory in heaven!

In the Himalayas a little flower is born. Forget-me-not. The glittering gaze of a star plays on it for an instant, and an answer is heard in a soft foreign tongue. *Myosotis!*

A silver pearl shone in the sands; a golden pearl sparkled in the sky... The world was created. Pure loves, divine sighs! Inflame the sacred mountain... for you have brothers in the valleys and in the bosom of the woods shy sisters are hiding.

Perfumed arbors of Paphos, you mean less to me than those places where the life-giving air of one's own country can be breathed in deeply. Over there, on the mountain tops, the world dwells content. The wild nightingale creates contentment!

Oh, how beautiful is my dear friend! She is so dear that she has pardoned the world, so kind she has pardoned me. The other night she was sleeping in some palace and I could not join her. My dark chestnut stallion slipped from beneath me. The broken reins streamed along its sweating flanks, and it required enormous efforts on my part to keep it from lying down on the ground.

That night Saturninus came to my assistance and my dear friend took her place at my side on her white mare caparisoned with silver. She said to me: "Courage, brother! This is the last stage of the journey." And her great eyes consumed space, and her long hair, full of the perfume of Yemen, floated in the air.

I recognized the beloved features of ***. We flew to our triumph and our enemies fell at our feet. The messenger hoopoe led us to the summit of the skies, and the bow of light shone in the sacred hands of Apollo. The enchanted horn of Adonis echoed through the woods.

O Death, where is thy victory, now that the all-conquering Messiah has ridden between us? His garment was of the color of hyacinth, and his wrists and ankles sparkled with diamonds and rubies. When his light switch touched the pearly gates of the New Jerusalem, we were all three bathed in light. It was then that I came down among men to give them the glad tidings.

I have come out of a very sweet dream. I saw the woman I loved, radiant and transfigured. Heaven opened in all its glory and I read the word *forgiveness* written in Christ's blood.

A star shone suddenly and revealed the secret of the world of worlds to me. Hosannah! Peace on earth and glory in heaven!

From the depths of the silent shadows two notes rang out, one low, one shrill — and the eternal orb immediately began to turn. Blessed be the first octave of the divine hymn! From Sabbath to Sabbath, let it enfold each day in its magic net. The hills sing of you to the valleys, the springs to the streams, the streams to the rivers, and the rivers to the sea; the air thrills, and light gently bursts the budding flowers. A sigh, a shiver of love comes from the swollen womb of earth, and the choir of stars unfolds itself in infinity;

it parts and returns again, contracts and expands, sowing in the remoteness of space the seeds of new creations.

On the crest of a bluish mountain a little flower is born. Forget-me-not. The glittering gaze of a star plays on it for an instant, and an answer is heard in a soft foreign tongue. *Myosotis!*

Woe to you, God of the North — who with one hammer blow broke the holy table, made of the seven most precious metals! For you could not break the *Rose Pearl* which reposed in its center. It rebounded under your iron — and here we are, armed for it... Hosannah!

The *macrocosm,* or greater world, was constructed by cabalistic art; the *microcosm,* or smaller world, is its image reflected in every heart. The Rose Pearl has been stained with the royal blood of the Valkyries. Woe to you, God of the Forge, for attempting to break the world!

But Christ's pardon was pronounced for you also.

Therefore blessed be thou, O giant Thor, Odin's most powerful son! Be blessed in Hela, your mother, for often death is sweet, and in your brother Loki, and in your hound Garnur!

The serpent which surrounds the world is itself blessed, for it is slackening its coils, and its yawning jaws breathe in the anxoka, the sulphurous flower, the bursting flower of the sun!

May God preserve sacred Balder, son of Odin, and the beautiful Freya!

★   ★   ★

I found myself *in spirit* at Saardam, which I visited last year. Snow lay on the ground. A little girl was walking and sliding over the icy surface towards, as I thought, the house of Peter the Great. Her proud profile had a Bourbon look. Her dazzlingly white neck slightly emerged from a cape of swan's feathers. With her little pink hand she sheltered a lighted lamp from the wind, and was about to knock on the green door of the house when a lean cat came out, entangled itself in her legs, and upset her.

"Why!" said the girl, getting up. "It's only a cat."

"Well, a cat is something after all," answered a soft voice.

I was present at this scene and I had in my arms a little grey cat which began to mew.

"It's that old fairy's child!" said the little girl. And she went into the house.

That night my dreams took me first to Vienna. Everyone knows that on each of the squares of this city there is one of those tall columns called *pardons*. Marble clouds are gathered to typify the order of Solomon, and to uphold the globes where seated divinities preside. Suddenly — oh, wonder! — I began to think of that august sister of the Emperor of Russia, whose imperial palace at Weimar I had seen. A fit of tender melancholy showed me the colored mists of a Norwegian landscape lit by a soft grey daylight. The clouds became transparent, and in front of me there opened an abyss into which rushed in tumult the frozen waves of the Baltic. It seemed that the whole of the Neva with its blue waters were to be swallowed up in this crack in the world. The ships of Cronstadt and Saint Petersburg bobbed at anchor, ready to break away and vanish in the gulf, when a divine radiance from above lighted up this scene of desolation.

In the bright beam of light piercing the mist, I saw the rock on which stands the statue of Peter the Great. Above this solid pedestal clouds rose in groups, piling up to the zenith. They were laden with radiant, heavenly forms, among which could be distinguished the two Catherines and the Empress Saint Helen, accompanied by the loveliest princesses of Muscovy and Poland. Their gentle expressions, directed towards France, lessened the distance by means of long crystal telescopes. By that I saw that our country had become the arbiter of the old quarrel of the East, and that they were awaiting its solution. My dream ended in the sweet hope that peace would at last be granted us.

In this way I urged myself on to a bold undertaking. I resolved to fix my dream-state and learn its secret. "Why should I not," I asked myself, "at last force those mystic gates, armed with all my will power, and dominate my sensations instead of being subject to them? Is it not possible to control this fascinating, dread chimera, to rule the spirits of the night which play with our reason? Sleep takes up a third of our lives. It consoles the sorrows of our days and the sorrow of their pleasures; but I have never felt any rest in sleep. For a few seconds I am numbed, then a new life begins, freed from the conditions of time and space, and doubtless similar to that state which awaits us after death. Who knows if there is not some link between those two existences and if it is not possible for the soul to unite them now?"

From that moment on I devoted myself to trying to find the meaning of my dreams, and this anxiety influenced my waking thoughts. I seemed to understand that there was a bond between the external and internal worlds: that only inattention or spiritual confusion distorted the outward affinities between them, — and this explained the strangeness of certain pictures, which are like grimacing reflections of real objects on a surface of troubled water.

Such were the inspirations of my nights; my days were spent quietly with the poor patients whom I had made my friends. The consciousness that henceforth I was purified from the faults of my past life gave me infinite mental delight; the certainty of immortality and of the coexistence of everyone I had loved was as it were, a material reality for me now, and I blessed the fraternal soul who had brought me back from the depths of despair to the clear paths of religion.

The poor lad from whom intelligent life had been so strangely withdrawn was so well cared for that gradually his torpor was overcome. I learnt that he had been born in the country and so spent whole hours singing him old village songs, which I tried to make as moving as possible. I had the happiness of seeing that he heard them, and he repeated certain parts of the songs. At last, one day, he opened his eyes for a second, and I saw that they were as blue as those of the Spirit who had appeared to me in my dream. One morning, some days later, he kept his eyes wide open and did not shut them. Then he began to speak, though only at intervals, and he recognized me and addressed me in a familiar way, calling me brother. However, he still could not get himself to eat. One day, coming in from the garden, he said to me: "I am thirsty."

I went and got him something to drink; the glass touched his lips but he could not swallow.

"Why," I asked him, "don't you want to eat and drink like other people?"

"Because I am dead," he answered. "I was buried in a certain graveyard, and in a certain place there…"

"And where do you suppose you are now?"

"In purgatory. I am undergoing my expiation."

Such are the odd ideas that come with that sort of sickness; I recognized that I myself had not been far from just such a strange belief. The way I had been cared for had already brought me back to the affection of family and friends, and I was able to judge with greater sanity the world of illusion in which I had lived for a little while. All the same, I feel happy over those convictions I have acquired, and I compare this series of trials I went through to that ordeal which, for the ancients, represented the idea of a descent into hell.

SYLVIE

RECOLLECTIONS OF VALOIS

I

A LOST NIGHT

I came out of a theater[1] where I used to spend every evening in the prosce-
nium boxes in the role of an ardent wooer. The theater was sometimes full,
sometimes empty. I myself cared little whether I saw stalls filled with thirty
amateurs brought in under duress and boxes filled with out-of-date hats and
dresses — or whether I were part of a house trembling with animation,
crowned at every level with flowering silks, glittering jewels, and radiant faces.
I was indifferent to what I saw in the house and the stage itself scarcely
attracted my attention until, in the second or third scene of some dismal
masterpiece of those days, a face I knew so well lit up the vacant boards and
gave life to the empty apparitions around me with the breath of a single
word.

    In her I felt myself alive, and she seemed to live for me alone. Her smile
filled me with infinite beatitude; her voice was so gentle and so vibrant, yet
strong in pitch, that I thrilled with joy and love. For me she was perfection,
she answered all my enthusiasms, every whim. She was as lovely as day itself
in the footlights that lit her from below, and pale as night when their dimmed
glare left her illumined from above by the rays of the chandelier and dis-
played her more naturally, shining in her own shadowed beauty, like the
divine Hours which stand out so clearly, with stars on their foreheads, against
the brown backgrounds of the frescoes at Herculaneum.

For a whole year I did not think of asking who she might be in real life. I was afraid to cloud the magic mirror which gave me her image — all I had heard was some gossip about the woman, rather than the actress. I took as little notice of it as of the rumors about the princess d'Élide or the queen of Trébizonde, for one of my uncles, who had lived through the end of the eighteenth century (and lived as one had to live, in those days), had early warned me that actresses were not women and that nature had denied them hearts. No doubt he spoke of the actresses of his own day, but he had told me so many stories of illusions and deceptions, shown me so many portraits on ivory (charming medallions which he subsequently used to decorate his snuffboxes), exhibited so many yellowing letters, such a heap of faded favors, telling me their history and final outcome, that I became accustomed to think ill of all actresses without making any allowance for changes in time.

We were then living in a strange period, such as usually succeeds revolutions or the decline of great reigns. It was no longer the gallant heroism of the Fronde, the elegant, dressed-up vice of the Regency, or the scepticism and insane orgies of the Directoire. It was an age in which activity, hesitation, and indolence were mixed up, together with dazzling Utopias, philosophies, and religious aspirations, vague enthusiasms, mild ideas of a Renaissance, weariness with past struggles, insecure optimisms — somewhat like the period of Peregrinus and Apuleius. Material man longed for the bouquet of roses which would regenerate him from the hands of the divine Isis; the goddess in her eternal youth and purity appeared to us by night and made us ashamed of our wasted days. We had not reached the age of ambition, and the greedy scramble for honors and positions caused us to stay away from all possible spheres of activity. The only refuge left to us was the poet's ivory tower, which we climbed, ever higher, to isolate ourselves from the mob.[2] Led by our masters to those high places we breathed at last the pure air of solitude, we drank oblivion in the legendary golden cup, and we got drunk on poetry and love. Love, however, of vague forms, of blue and rosy hues, of metaphysical phantoms! Seen at close quarters, the real woman revolted our ingenuous souls. She had to be a queen or goddess; above all, she had to be unapproachable.

Yet some of us were not entirely taken with these Platonic paradoxes, and through our renewed reveries of Alexandria we occasionally waved the torch of the underground gods that lights the darkness for a moment with its trail of sparks. So, coming out of the theater in the bitter sadness of my vanished dream, I gladly joined a group which used to dine together in some numbers, and with whom every melancholy was dissipated by the inexhaustible energy of a few brilliant minds. These lively, wild, frequently sublime minds are invariably to be found at times of renaissance or decadence, and our discussions achieved such heights that the more fearful among us used to look out of the windows to see whether the Huns, Tartars, or Cossacks were not on the way to cut short these arguments of sophists and rhetoricians.

"Wine, woman — there you have wisdom!" Such was the sentiment of one of our younger members. Someone said to me: "For some time now I've been meeting you in the same theater, every time I go there. Which of them do you go for?"

Which! It seemed to me impossible to go there for any other. However I let slip a name.

"Well," my friend said, indulgently, "over there sits the happy man who has just taken her home and who, according to the rules of our club, probably won't go to her again until the night is over."

Without much emotion I looked at the man indicated. He was young, well dressed, with a pale, nervous face, good manners, and eyes marked by melancholy and tenderness. He was throwing money on a table of whist and losing it with indifference.

"What does it matter to me," I said. "He, or somebody else. There had to be some man, and he seems to me worthy of her choice."

"What about you then?"

"Me? I pursue an image, no more."

As I went out I passed through the reading room and looked mechanically at a newspaper to see, I think it was, the state of the stock market. Among the ruins of my fortune there was a fair amount in foreign bonds. There had been a rumor that after having been passed over for several years they were about to be recognized; this had resulted from a change of ministry. The bonds were already quoted high. I was rich again.

Only one thought came into my mind at this change in my circumstances — that the woman I had been in love with for so long was mine if I liked. My finger touched my ideal. But was it not just another illusion, a mocking printer's misprint? No. The other newspaper confirmed it. The sum I had gained reared itself before me like a golden Moloch. I thought: "What would that young man say if I were to go and take his place beside the lady he has left alone?" I shuddered at the idea. My pride revolted.

No! Not like this! A man cannot kill love with gold at my age! I will not be a corrupter. Besides, this is a notion from another age. Who can say that this woman is venal? My glance strayed vaguely through the newspaper in my hand and I read these two lines: *"Fête du Bouquet provincial. —* Tomorrow the archers of Senlis are to return the bouquet to the archers of Loisy."[3] These extremely simple words aroused in me a whole new set of impressions, a memory of country life I had long ago forgotten, a distant echo of the simple festivals of my childhood. Horn and drum resounded far off in the woods and hamlets, the girls were weaving garlands and arranging, as they sang, bouquets tied in ribbons. A heavy cart, drawn by oxen, took their gifts as it passed, and we, the children of the district, formed the escort with our bows and arrows, dignifying ourselves with the title of knights — without realizing that we were simply repeating from age to age a Druid festival that had survived the new monarchies and the novel religions.

II

ADRIENNE

I went to bed but could not rest. Lost in a kind of half-sleep, all my youth passed through my memory again. This state, when the spirit still resists the strange combinations of dreams, often allows us to compress into a few moments the most salient pictures of a long period of life.[4]

I fancied for myself a château of the time of Henry IV,[5] with its pointed roofs covered with slates, its ruddy facade and coigns of yellow stone, and a large green space framed in elms and lime trees, their leaves pierced by the fiery shafts of a setting sun. On the lawn some girls were doing a round dance and singing old airs handed down to them by their mothers in such a naturally pure French you felt that this was indeed that old country of Valois, where the heart of France has been beating for more than a thousand years.

I was the only boy in the round, and I had brought with me my young companion, Sylvie, a little girl from the next village, bright and fresh, with black eyes, a regular profile, and lightly tanned skin... I loved her alone, she was the only one I had eyes for — until then! In the round we were dancing I had barely noticed a tall, lovely, fair-haired girl they called Adrienne. All at once, in accordance with the rules of the dance, Adrienne and I found ourselves alone in the center of the circle. We were of the same height. We were told to kiss and the dancing and the chorus whirled around us more quickly than ever. As I gave her this kiss I could not resist pressing her hand. The long tight curls of her golden hair brushed my cheeks and from that moment on an inexplicable confusion took hold of me.

The girl had to sing a song in order to regain her place in the dance. We sat around her and straight away, in a fresh, penetrating, slightly filmy voice, like a true daughter of that misty region, she sang one of those old ballads, full of melancholy and love, which always tell of the sufferings of a princess confined in a tower by her father as a punishment for having fallen in love. The melody ended at each stanza in those wavering trills which show off young voices so well, especially when, in a controlled tremor, they imitate the quavering tones of old women.

As she sang, the shadows came down from the great trees, and the first moonlight fell on her as she stood alone in our attentive circle. She stopped, and no one dared to break the silence. The lawn was covered with thin veils of vapor which trailed white tufts on the tips of the grasses. We imagined we were in paradise. Finally I got up and ran to the gardens of the château, where some laurels grew, planted in large faïence vases with monochrome bas-reliefs. I brought back two branches which were then woven into a crown and tied with a ribbon. This I put on Adrienne's head and glistening leaves shone on her fair hair in the pale moonlight. She was like Dante's Beatrice, smiling on the poet as he strayed on the verge of the blessed abodes.

Adrienne rose. Showing off her slender figure she made us a graceful bow and ran back to the château. They said she was the grandchild of one of the descendants of a family related to the ancient kings of France. The blood of the house of Valois flowed in her veins. For this one day of festival she had been allowed to mix in our games; but we were not to see her again, for the next morning she returned to the convent where she was a boarder.

When I got back to Sylvie I saw she was crying. Her tears were on account of the crown that my hands had given the fair singer. I offered to go and gather another for her, but she said she would not consider it, she was not worthy of one. I tried to excuse myself in vain, she did not speak a word to me the whole of the way home.

I myself was called back to Paris to continue my studies and I bore with me this double image — of a tender friendship sadly broken, and of a vague, impossible love, one that caused me painful thoughts impossible to assuage in college philosophy.

The figure of Adrienne alone remained triumphant, a mirage of fortune and beauty, sharing my hours of heavy study and making them sweeter. During my next year's vacation I learnt that this lovely creature, whom I had scarcely seen, was consecrated to a nun's life by her family.

III

RESOLUTION

Everything was explained to me by this half-dreamed memory. That impalpable and hopeless love I had conceived for a woman of the theater, that love which seized me each evening when the curtain went up, and left me alone only in sleep, this had its seed in the memory of Adrienne, a flower of the night efflorescent in the moon's pale glimmer, flesh-colored and fair phantom gliding over the green grasses half-bathed in whitish vapors. The likeness of this long forgotten figure was now drawn before me with a curious clarity; it was a pencil drawing blurred by time that had been converted into a picture, like those old sketches of the masters you admire in some museum and then you find, somewhere else, the dazzling original.

To love a nun in the form of an actress!... but what if they were one and the same! — It was enough to drive you mad! That fascination is fatal in which the unknown leads you on like a will-o'-the-wisp hovering over the reeds in still water... But let us get back to reality.

Why have I for three years forgotten Sylvie, whom I loved so much?... She was a very pretty girl, the loveliest in Loisy.

She is still alive, good and purehearted, no doubt. Once more I can see her window with the grapevines enlaced among the roses, and the cage of linnets hung up on the left. I hear the sound of her sonorous spindles and her favorite song:

> *The fair lady is sitting*
> *Beside the swift stream...*

She is waiting for me. Who would marry Sylvie? She is so poor. In her village, and those nearby, there are good peasants, dressed in smocks, with horny hands, lean faces, and sunburnt skins. She loved only me, the little Parisian, who went to Loisy to see his poor uncle, now dead. For three years I have frittered away in lordly fashion the little he left me, which would have been enough for my whole life. With Sylvie I would have kept it. Now good luck has given me back some of it. There is still time.

What is she doing at this moment? Is she asleep?... No, she is not asleep; today is the festival of the bow, the only celebration of the year when you dance all night.[6] She's there.

What time is it?

I had no watch.

In the midst of all the bric-a-brac splendors which it was then the custom to collect to give local color to an old-fashioned apartment, there shone the restored brilliance of a tortoiseshell Renaissance timepiece. Its gilded dome, surmounted by the figure of Time, was supported by caryatids in the Medici manner, resting in their turn on rearing horses. The historical figure of Diana, leaning on her stag, was in low relief under the face on which the enameled figures of the hours were displayed on an inlaid background. The works, excellent ones, no doubt, had not been wound up for two centuries. I had not bought that clock in Touraine to tell the time.

I went down to the concierge. The cuckoo clock there told me it was one in the morning. — "In four hours," I said to myself, "I can be at the ball at Loisy."

There were still five or six cabs on the Place du Palais Royal, waiting for the habitués of clubs and gambling houses.

"To Loisy," I said to the first.

"Where' s that?"

"Near Senlis. Eight leagues."

"I'll take you to the coach-office," said the driver, who was less concerned than I was.

What a dreary track that Flanders road is at night. It only becomes beautiful when you reach the forest region. All the time those two lines of monotonous trees, grimacing in vague shapes; beyond them, square slabs of green, and of ploughed earth, bounded on the left by the bluish hills of Montmorency, Écouen, and Luzarches. Here is Gonesse, a vulgar little town full of memories of the Ligue and the Fronde...

Beyond Louvres is a road lined with apple trees whose blossoms I saw so many times gleaming in the night like earthbound stars; it was the shortest way to reach the hamlets. — As the carriage climbs the hillsides, let us reconstruct the memories of the time I went there so often.

IV

A VOYAGE TO CYTHERA[7]

Some years had gone by. The time when I had met Adrienne in front of the château was already only a memory of childhood. I was at Loisy once again, at the time of the annual festival. Once again I joined the knights of the bow and took my place in the company I had been part of before. The festival had been organized by young people from the old families who still own some of those old châteaux hidden in the forest there, and these mansions have suffered more from time than from revolutions. From Chantilly,

Compiègne, and Senlis flocked happy cavalcades to take their places in the rustic procession of the companies of the bow. After the long walk through the villages and little towns, after Mass in the church, after the trials of skill and the prize-giving, the winners were invited to a banquet given on an island shaded by limes and poplars, in the middle of one of those pools fed by the Nonette and the Thève. Beflagged boats bore us to the island, which had been selected because of the existence on it of an oval temple with columns that could serve as banquet hall. There, as at Ermenonville, the countryside is dotted with those light, late eighteenth-century edifices that philosophical millionaires were inspired to plan after the dominant taste of their day. I think this temple must have originally been dedicated to Urania. Three columns had collapsed and carried down part of the architrave in their fall; but the interior of the hall had been swept, garlands had been hung between the columns, and a new youth had been given this modern ruin that belonged to the paganism of Boufflers and Chaulieu rather than to that of Horace.

Perhaps the crossing of the lake had been devised in order to recall Watteau's *Voyage à Cythère.* Only our modern clothes spoiled the illusion. The immense festival bouquet had been taken from the cart that carried it and placed in a large boat; the train of young girls dressed in white, who accompanied it according to custom, sat on the benches, and this graceful *theoria,* a revival from the days of antiquity, was reflected in the calm waters of the pool separating it from the banks of the island, so rose-colored in the evening sun with its thorn thickets, its colonnade, and clear foliage. All the boats soon reached land. The flower basket, ceremoniously carried, occupied the center of the table and everyone sat down, the most favored men next to the girls. For this you only had to know their parents. That was why I found myself next to Sylvie. Her brother had met me during the festival and made fun of my not having visited their family for so long. I pleaded my studies in Paris as excuse and assured him that I had come for that very reason.

"No," said Sylvie, "he's forgotten me. We are village folk, and Paris is far above us."

I tried to close her mouth with a kiss, but she went on pouting at me, and her brother had to intervene to get her even to hold out her cheek to me in an indifferent way. I had no pleasure in this kiss, a favor that many others obtained, for in such a patriarchal district, where every passer-by is greeted, a kiss is no more than a mark of politeness among honest folk.

A surprise had been arranged by those who had organized the festival. At the end of the meal we saw a wild swan, which had been held captive under the flowers until then, fly up from the depths of the huge basket. With its strong wings it lifted up a tangle of garlands and crowns of flowers, finally dispersing them on all sides. While the bird flew joyfully into the last gleams of the sun, we caught the flower-crowns at random and each man instantly decorated the brow of the girl beside him. I was lucky enough to get one of the finest and, smiling, Sylvie this time allowed me to kiss her more tenderly than before. I understood that I had thus erased the memory of another occasion. My admiration for her at this moment was undivided, she had become so beautiful! She was no longer the little village girl I had scorned for someone older and more schooled in the graces of society. Everything about her had improved. The charm of her black eyes, so seductive in childhood, had become irresistible; under the arched orbit of her eyebrows her smile had something Athenian about it as it suddenly illumined her regular and placid features. I admired this countenance, worthy of antique art in the midst of the irregular baby-faces of her companions. Her delicately tapering hands, her arms which had grown whiter as they rounded, her lithe figure, all made her quite another creature from the girl I had seen before. I could not resist telling her how different from her old self I now found her, hoping in this way to cover over my former, rapid infidelity.

Everything else, too, was in my favor, her brother's friendship for me, the enchanting impression of the festival, the evening hour and even the place, where, by a phantasy in happy taste, had been reproduced an image of the stately gallantry of old times. As often as we could we escaped from the dancing to talk about our recollections of childhood and to dream together admiring the sky's reflection on the dark leaves and still waters. Sylvie's brother had to tear us away from this meditation by telling us it was time to return to the somewhat distant village where their parents lived.

V

THE VILLAGE

They lived in the old keeper's lodge at Loisy. I went back with them and then returned to Montagny, where I was staying with my uncle. I left the road to cross a small wood separating Loisy from Saint-S*** and soon plunged into a sunken path that skirts the forest of Ermenonville; I then expected to strike the walls of a convent which one has to follow for a quarter of a league. From time to time the moon was hidden by clouds and scarcely showed up the dark sandstone rocks and the heather that became more abundant as I advanced. To right and left were fringes of woods with no marked paths, and always ahead of me rose the Druidical rocks of the district, which still guarded the memory of the sons of Armen whom the Romans put to death. From the top of these sublime masses I saw the distant pools stand out like mirrors on the misty plain, but I could not tell which one it was where the festival had been held.

The air was warm and perfumed; I decided to go no further, but to lie down on the heather and wait for morning. When I woke up, I gradually recognized the points near the spot where I had lost my way in the night. To my left I saw the long line of the walls of the convent of Saint-S***,[8] the Gens d'Armes hills, with the shattered ruins of the old Carolingian palace. Near it, above the tops of the trees, the tall ruins of the Abbey of Thiers outlined against the horizon its broken walls pierced with trefoils and ogives. Further on, the manor house of Pontarmé, still surrounded by its moat, began to reflect the first light of day, while to the south the tall keep of La Tournelle and the four towers of Bertrand-Fosse rose up on the first slopes of Montméliant.

The night had been dear to me and I thought only of Sylvie. Still, the sight of the convent gave me the idea for a moment that possibly it was the one where Adrienne was. The chimes of the matin bell were still in my ears, and had no doubt awakened me. For an instant I had the notion of climbing the highest point of the rocks and peering over its walls; but on reflection I stopped myself — it would have been a profanation. The dawning day banished this vain memory from my mind and left only the fresh features of Sylvie.

"I'll go and wake her up," I said to myself, and continued on my way to Loisy.

There stood the village at the end of the path round the wood — twenty thatched cottages, their walls covered with climbing roses and vines. Some early women wool spinners, red handkerchiefs around their heads, were already working together in front of a farm. Sylvie was not among them. Since she has learnt to make fine lace she has become quite a lady, while her parents remain simple villagers. Without causing any surprise I went up to her room; she had already been up for some time and was moving her lace bobbins which made a gentle clicking on the green cushion resting on her knees.

"So there you are, lazybones," she said, with her divine smile, "I'm certain you've only just got out of bed."

I told her of the sleepless night I had spent and of my wanderings among the woods and rocks when I had lost my way. She sympathized with me for a moment.

"If you don't feel too tired, I'll take you on some more wanderings. We'll go and see my great-aunt at Othys."

I had scarcely replied when she jumped up joyously, arranged her hair in front of a mirror, and put on a country straw hat. Innocence and joy leapt from her eyes. We started out, following the Thève, across meadows sown with buttercups and daisies, then along the Saint-Laurent woods, from time to time crossing streams and hedges to shorten the way. Blackbirds sang in the trees and when we brushed the bushes blue tits flew gaily away.

Now and again we came across those periwinkle trailers so beloved of Rousseau, their blue corollas open in the long tendrils of coupled leaves, humble creepers that hindered my companion's nimble feet. Indifferent to memories of the philosopher of Geneva, she looked here and there for scented strawberries while I talked to her of *la Nouvelle Héloïse*, several passages of which I recited by heart.

"Is it pretty?" she asked.

"Sublime."

"Is it better than Auguste Lafontaine?"[9]

"More tender."

"Oh well," she said, "I must read it. I shall tell my brother to bring it me the next time he goes in to Senlis."

And I continued to quote fragments of *Héloïse* while Sylvie gathered strawberries.

VI

OTHYS

As we came out of the wood, we found large clumps of purple foxglove; she picked a big bunch and said, "For my aunt. She'll be so happy to have these lovely flowers in her room."

We had only a short stretch of level ground to cross before reaching Othys. The village steeple soared above the bluish hills which run from Montméliant to Dammartin. The Thève once again rippled over rocks and pebbles, narrowing as it neared its source, where it slumbers in the meadows, spreading into a little lake surrounded by gladioli and irises. Soon we reached the first houses. Sylvie's aunt lived in a little thatched cottage built of irregular pieces of sandstone trellised with hops and virgin vines. She lived alone on a few acres of land which the village folk had farmed for her since her husband's death. A visit from her niece always put the house in a turmoil.

"Good morning, Aunt," exclaimed Sylvie. "Here are your children. And very hungry." She kissed her aunt tenderly, placed the bunch of flowers in her arms, then, remembering to introduce me, said, "This is my sweetheart!"

I, in turn, kissed her aunt who said, "He's nice... So he's fair-haired!"

"He's got nice fine hair," Sylvie said.

"That won't last long," her aunt replied, "but you have plenty of time in front of you, and you're dark, you'll go together very well."

"We must get him something to eat, Aunt," said Sylvie. And she began looking in the cupboards and pantry, where she found milk, bread and sugar, and laid the table, without too much order, with plates and dishes of earthenware decorated with large flowers and cocks of brilliant plumage. A bowl of Creil porcelain, in which strawberries were swimming in milk, was made the centerpiece, and, after she had stolen a few fistfuls of cherries and gooseberries from the garden, she put two vases of flowers at either end of the cloth. But her aunt made the excellent remark: "That can do for dessert. Now you let me get to work."

She unhooked the frying pan and flung a bundle of wood into the high fireplace. "I don't want you to touch it," she told Sylvie who was anxious to help her. "Think of spoiling those pretty fingers which can make finer lace than they do at Chantilly! You gave me some and I know what lace is."

"Oh, yes, Aunt... If you have any old pieces, I could use them as patterns."

"Well, go and look upstairs," she answered. "There may be some in my chest of drawers."

"Can I have the keys then?" Sylvie asked.

"Bah!" replied her aunt. "All the drawers are open."

"That's not true, there's one that's always kept locked." And while the good lady was cleaning the frying pan after having warmed it over the fire,

Sylvie took off her aunt's belt a little key of chased steel and held it up to me triumphantly.

I followed her quickly up the wooden stairs that led to the bedroom. O sacred youth, O holy old age! Who could ever have thought of sullying the purity of a first love in such a sanctuary of faithful memories? In an oval gilt frame, hung at the head of the rustic bed, the portrait of a young man of the good old times smiled from dark eyes and fresh lips. He wore the uniform of a gamekeeper of the House of Condé; his semimilitary bearing, his rosy, kindly face, his candid forehead under the powdered hair, enhanced this probably mediocre pastel with the graces of youth and simplicity. Some unknown artist, invited to join the hunting parties of the prince, had done his best to portray the keeper and his young bride, who could be seen in another medallion, attractive and mischievous-looking, lissome in her open corset laced with ribbons, and teasing, with her pert profile, a bird perched on her finger. It was the same good old lady, however, who was at that moment bent over the hearth cooking. I could not help thinking of the Funambules fairies[10] who put wrinkled masks over their own charming faces, which they uncover at the end of the piece when the temple of Love appears with its whirling sun shining with magic fires.

"Oh, dear aunt," I cried out, "how lovely you used to be."

"And what about me?" asked Sylvie, who had succeeded in opening the famous drawer. In it she had found a great dress of flame-colored taffeta, whose folds rustled loudly. "I must see if it fits," she said. "I shall look like an old fairy."

"The ever-young fairy of myth," was what I said to myself. Sylvie had already undone her own muslin dress and let it slip to her feet. Her old aunt's

dress, rich in material, fitted Sylvie's slender figure perfectly and she told me
to hook it up for her.

"Oh! These straight sleeves look quite ridiculous," she said. Yet the lace-
edged sleeves showed off her bare arms splendidly, her breasts being framed
in the corsage of yellow tulle and faded ribbons which had so little held in
her aunt's vanished charms.

"Come on, hurry up! Don't you know how to hook up a girl's dress yet?"
Sylvie said to me. She looked like Greuze's *Village Bride*.

"You need powder," I said. "We must find some."

She rummaged again through the drawers. What riches were there! How
good it all smelled, how it shone and glittered with brilliant colors and
humble tinsel! Two mother-of-pearl fans, slightly broken, pots with Chinese
subjects on them, an amber necklace and a thousand trifles among which
shone two little white wool slippers, their buckles encrusted with paste
diamonds!

"Oh, I must put them on," Sylvie cried, "if only I can find the embroi-
dered stockings."

A moment later we unrolled some silk stockings of a delicate rose color
with green clocks; but her aunt's voice, accompanied by a sizzling from the
pan, suddenly brought us back to reality.

"Quick," said Sylvie, "you go on down." And in spite of all I could say
she would not let me help her on with her shoes and stockings. Meanwhile
her aunt was turning out the contents of the pan on to a dish — a slice of
bacon and some eggs. Sylvie's call soon brought me back to her.

"Get dressed quickly!" she said. She herself was fully dressed and she
showed me the keeper's wedding costume all put out on the chest of drawers.

In a moment I had turned myself into the bridegroom of the previous century. Sylvie was waiting for me on the stairs and we went down together, hand in hand.

Her aunt turned and saw us and gave a start. "Oh, my children!" she said and began to cry, soon smiling through her tears. It was the image of her own youth, a vision at once cruel and charming. We sat down beside her, touched and almost grave. But soon our gay spirits came back to us as, the first shock over, the dear old soul could think of nothing else but recounting the stately ceremonies of her own wedding. She even discovered in her memory those alternating songs, then customary, which went from one end of the nuptial table to the other, and the simple epithalamion which accompanied the young couple as they went home after the dance. We repeated the artless rhythms of these verses, with the pauses and assonances of their time, flowery and passionate like the Song of Songs. We were the bride and bridegroom for a whole summer morning.

VII

CHÂALIS

It is four in the morning; the road plunges into a dip of land and then rises again. The carriage is going by Orry, then on to La Chapelle. To the left there is a road that runs along the wood of Hallate. It was along there that Sylvie's brother drove me one evening in his little cart to a country ceremony. It was, I believe, Saint Bartholomew's Eve. His little horse flew through the woods and unfrequented roads as if to some witches' Sabbath. We reached the paved road again at Mont l'Évêque and a few minutes later stopped at the keeper's lodge at the ancient Abbey of Châalis — Châalis, yet another memory!

This former retreat of emperors now merely offers for our admiration the ruins of its cloisters with their Byzantine arcades, the last of which still stands out reflected in the pools — a forgotten fragment of those pious foundations included in the properties that used to be called "the farms of Charlemagne." In this district, cut off from the movement of roads and cities, religion has preserved especial traces of the long stay made there by the Cardinals of the House of Este in the times of the Medici; its customs and emblems still retain something gallant and poetic, you breathe a perfume of the Renaissance beneath the chapel arches with their slender moldings, decorated by Italian artists. The figures of saints and angels are silhouetted in rose on vaults of a delicate blue and carry an air of pagan allegory that reminds one of the sentimentalities of Petrarch and of the fabulous mysticism of Francesco Colonna.[11]

We were intruders, Sylvie's brother and I, in the private festival that took place that night. A personage of very noble birth, who at that time owned the estate, had had the idea of inviting several families of the district to a sort of allegorical representation, in which some of the pupils of the neighboring convent were to take part. It was no imitation of the tragedies of Saint-Cyr but went back to the first lyric attempt introduced into France at the time of the Valois. What I saw performed was like a mystery play of ancient times. The costumes were long robes, varied only in their colors, of azure, hyacinth, and of the color of dawn. The action took place among angels, on the ruins of the shattered world. Each voice sang one of the splendors of this vanished world, and the angel of death declared the causes of its destruction. A spirit arose from the abyss, holding in its hand a flaming sword, and summoned the others to come and adore the glory of Christ, the conqueror of hell. This spirit was Adrienne, transfigured by her costume as she already was by her vocation. The halo of gilt cardboard around her angelic head seemed to us, quite naturally, a circle of light; her voice had gained in strength and range, and the endless *fioriture* of Italian singing embroidered the severe phrases of stately recitative with their birdlike trills.

As I retrace these details I have to ask myself if they were real or if I dreamed them. Sylvie's brother was a little drunk that evening. For a while we stopped at the keeper's house — where I was greatly struck to see a swan with spread wings displayed above the door, and inside some tall cupboards of carved walnut, a large clock in its case, and trophies of bows and arrows of honor over a red and green target. An odd dwarf, wearing a Chinese cap, and holding a bottle in one hand and a ring in the other, seemed to be inviting the marksmen to aim true. The dwarf, I am sure, was cut out of sheet-iron. But is the apparition of Adrienne as real as these details, as real as the indisputable existence of the Abbey of Châalis? Yet I am certain it was the keeper's son who took us into the hall where the play took place; we were near the door, behind a large audience, who were seated and seemed deeply moved. It was Saint Bartholomew's Day — a day singularly connected with memories of the Medici, whose arms, impaled with those of the House of Este, decorated those old walls... Perhaps this memory is an obsession! Luckily the carriage stops here on the road to Plessis; I escape from the realm of reverie and have only a quarter of an hour's walk over little-used paths to reach Loisy.

VIII

THE BALL AT LOISY

I entered the ball at Loisy at that melancholy yet still gentle hour when the lights grow pale and tremble at the approach of day. The lime trees, in deep shadow at their roots, took on a bluish tint at the top. The bucolic flute no longer struggled so keenly with the song of the nightingale. Everyone looked pale and in the disheveled groups I had difficulty in finding faces I knew. At last I saw Lise, a friend of Sylvie. She kissed me.

"It's been a long time since we've seen you, Parisian!" she said.

"Yes, a long time."

"And you arrive at an hour like this?"

"I came by the coach."

"None too quickly."

"I wanted to see Sylvie. Is she still at the ball?"

"She never leaves until dawn. She likes dancing so much."

In an instant I was at her side. Her face seemed tired, but her black eyes still shone with the Athenian smile of old. A young man stood near her. She made a sign to him that she would not take the next dance. He bowed and went away.

Day was breaking. We left the ball, hand in hand. The flowers hung in Sylvie's undone hair; the bunch at her breast drooped also on her rumpled lace, the skillful work of her own fingers. I offered to take her home. It was now broad daylight, but the sky was overcast. The Thève murmured on our left, leaving pools of still water at each winding in its course, and here white and yellow water lilies bloomed and the frail embroidery of the water flowers spread out like daisies. The fields were covered with stooks and hayricks, whose odor went to my head without inebriation, as had at other times the fresh scent of the woods and thorn thickets.

We had no intention of crossing these again.

"Sylvie," I said, "you don't love me any more."

She sighed. "My friend," she said, "one has to find some reason. Things don't go as we want them to in life. Once you spoke to me of *la Nouvelle Héloïse*; I read it, and shivered as I came straight away on the sentence — 'Every young girl who reads this book is lost.'[12] Yet I read on, relying on my judgment. Do you remember the day we put on my aunt's wedding clothes?... The illustrations in the book also showed lovers in the old costumes of past days, so that for me you were Saint-Preux, and I saw myself in Julie. Ah! Why didn't you come back to me then? But they said you were in Italy.[13] You must have seen far prettier girls than me there!"

"Not one, Sylvie, with a look like yours, not one with the pure outline of your face. You are an antique nymph without knowing it. Besides, the woods of this district are as beautiful as those of the Roman Campagna. There are masses of granite no less sublime here, and a waterfall that cascades over the rocks like the one at Terni. I saw nothing there that I can regret here."

"And in Paris?" she said.

"In Paris..."

I shook my head without answering. Then suddenly I thought of the empty image which had led me astray for so long.

"Sylvie," I cried, "may we stop here?"

I threw myself at her feet. Weeping warm tears I confessed my irresolutions, my caprices. I described the fatal specter who had crossed my life.

"Save me," I concluded, "I am coming back to you forever."

She looked at me tenderly... At that moment our conversation was interrupted by violent shouts of laughter. Sylvie's brother rejoined us. He was bubbling over with that good country fun which always follows a night of festival and which copious refreshments had developed beyond measure. He called up the young gallant of the ball, who was hiding in the thorn bushes a little way away but who lost no time in joining us. This lad was scarcely any firmer on his feet than his friend, and seemed still more embarrassed by the presence of a Parisian than by Sylvie's. His open face, his deference mingled with embarrassment, prevented me from any annoyance with him I might have felt for his role of dancer on whose account they had stayed so long at the ball. I did not consider him very dangerous.

"We must go home," Sylvie said to her brother. "We'll meet soon," she said to me, offering her cheek.

The lover was not offended.

IX

ERMENONVILLE

I had no wish to sleep. I went to Montagny to revisit my uncle's house. A great sadness came over me when I caught sight of its yellow front and green shutters. Everything seemed to be in the same state as of old; only, I had to go to the farmer's to get the key of the front door. When the shutters had been opened I looked affectionately at the old furniture preserved in the same state and rubbed up from time to time, the tall walnut-wood cupboard, two Flemish paintings said to be the work of an ancient painter, an ancestor of

ours, large engravings after Boucher, and a whole series of framed illustra-
tions from *Émile* and *la Nouvelle Héloïse* by Moreau; on the table was a stuffed
dog which I had known alive as the old friend of my wanderings through the
woods, the last King Charles perhaps, for it belonged to that lost breed.

"The parrot is still living," the farmer informed me. "I've taken him
home with me."

The garden presented a wonderful picture of wild vegetation. In one
corner I recognized the child's garden I had laid out in the past. With a shud-
der I entered the study where there was still a small library of choice books,
old friends of the man who was now dead. On the desk there lay some
ancient relics discovered in his garden: vases, and Roman medals, a local
collection that had given him happiness.

"Let's go and see the parrot," I said to the farmer. The parrot asked for
food as it had done in its happiest days, and looked at me with its round eye,
bordered by wrinkled skin, which reminds you of the experienced look of an
old man.

Filled with the sad ideas recalled by this late visit to such beloved spots,
I felt I had to see Sylvie again, the only living and still youthful face that
linked me to the district. I took the road to Loisy again. It was noon; every-
one was asleep, tired from the festival. Ermenonville is about a league away
by the forest road and I suddenly had the idea that it would distract me
to walk there. It was fine summer weather. At first I delighted in the coolness
of this road which seemed like the avenue of a park. The great oaks of a
uniform green were only varied by the white trunks of the birches with their
quivering leaves. The birds were silent and the only sound I heard was that of
the woodpecker tapping the trees to hollow out its nest. For a moment I was

nearly lost, for the signposts marking the different roads in various places had lost their lettering. Finally, leaving the "Desert" to my left, I arrived at the dancing-ring where the old men's bench still remains. All the memories of philosophical antiquity, revived by the former owner of the estate, crowded back on me at the sight of this picturesque illustration of *Anacharsis* and *Émile.*

When I saw the waters of the lake glittering through the branches of the hazels and willows, I completely recognized a spot to which my uncle had often taken me on our walks: it was the "temple of Philosophy" which its originator had not been fortunate enough to finish. It is shaped like the temple of the Sybil and, still erect under the shelter of a clump of pines, displays the names of all great thinkers from Montaigne and Descartes to Rousseau.[14] This unfinished building is already no more than a ruin, with ivy gracefully festooning it, and the brambles invading its broken steps. As a child I had seen there those festivals at which girls dressed in white came to receive prizes for study and good conduct. Where are the rosebushes which surrounded the hill? The eglantine and wild raspberry hide the last of them, reverting to their wild state. As for the laurels, have they been cut down — as we learn from the song of the girls who do not want to return to the woods? No, those shrubs from gentle Italy have died under our misty skies. Fortunately the privet of Virgil still flourishes, as if to support the master's words inscribed above the door — *Rerum cognoscere causas.* Yes, this temple is falling like so many others, and man, tired or forgetful, has turned away from its threshold, while indifferent nature will reconquer the soil that art took from her; but the thirst for knowledge will live on forever, the source of all strength and activity.

Here are the island poplars and the tomb of Rousseau, empty of his ashes. O wise man! You gave us the milk of the strong and we were too feeble to profit from it. We have forgotten your lessons, which our fathers knew, and we have lost the meaning of your words, the last echo of ancient wisdom. But do not let us despair and, as you did at your last moment, let us turn our eyes to the sun!

I saw the château again, the peaceful waters surrounding it, the waterfall murmuring among the rocks, and that raised walk connecting the two parts of the village, marked with four dovecotes at its corners, and the lawn that stretches out beyond like a savanna overlooked by shady slopes; Gabrielle's tower is reflected from afar in the waters of an artificial lake, starry with ephemeral flowers; the water foams, the insects hum... You must shun the treacherous air it exhales and gain the dusty rocks of the "Desert" and then the moors where the purple broom relieves the green of the ferns. How solitary it all is and how sad! Sylvie's enchanting gaze, her wild running, her happy cries, once gave such charm to the places I have just been through. She was still a wild child, her feet were bare, her skin sunburnt in spite of the straw hat whose long ribbon streamed out carelessly with the tresses of her black hair. We used to go and drink milk at the Swiss farm, and they told me: "What a pretty sweetheart you have there, little Parisian!" Oh! No peasant boy would have danced with her then! She only danced with me, once a year, at the festival of the bow.

X

BIG CURLY

Again I took the road to Loisy; everyone was up. Sylvie was dressed like a fine lady, practically in the city fashion. She took me up to her room with all her old ingenuousness. Her eye still sparkled with a charming smile, but the marked arch of her eyebrows gave her from time to time a serious look. The room was simply decorated, though the furniture was modern; a gilt-edged mirror had replaced the old wall-glass where an idyllic shepherd offered a nest to a blue and pink shepherdess. The fourposter bed, chastely draped with old flowered chintz, had been succeeded by a walnut-wood bed hung with a net curtain; in the cage by the window there were canaries where there had once been linnets. I was anxious to leave the room, for it contained nothing of the past.

"You're not working at your lace today?" I asked Sylvie.

"Oh, I don't make lace any more, there's no demand for it in the country; even at Chantilly the factory is closed."

"What do you do, then?"

She went to a corner of the room and produced an iron instrument that looked like a long pair of pliers.

"What's that?"

"They call it the 'mechanic'; it's for holding the leather of gloves while they're being sewn."

"Ah! So you are a glove-maker, Sylvie?"

"Yes. We work for Dammartin here, it's paying well at present; but I'm not doing anything today; let's go where you like."

I turned my eyes in the direction of the road to Othys; she shook her head; I realized that her old aunt was no longer alive. Sylvie called up a little boy and made him saddle a donkey.

"I'm still tired from yesterday," she said, "but the ride will do me good;

let's go to Châalis."

And so there we were crossing the forest, followed by the little boy carrying a switch. Sylvie soon wanted to rest and I kissed her as I urged her to sit down. Our conversation could no longer be very intimate. I had to tell her of my life in Paris, of my travels...

"How can anyone travel so far?" she said

"I am surprised myself when I see you again."

"Oh, you just say that!"

"You must admit you weren't so pretty in those days."

"That I don't know."

"Do you remember the time when we were children, and you the bigger?"

"And you the cleverer!"

"Oh, Sylvie!"

"They put us in the donkey's panniers, one each side."

"And we called each other 'thou'... Do you remember teaching me to catch fresh-water shrimps under the bridges over the Thève and the Nonette?"

"And do you remember your foster brother one day pulling you out of the 'waater,' as he called it?"

"Big Curly! It was he who told me I could get across the 'waater.' "

I quickly changed the conversation. This recollection had vividly recalled the time when I visited the district, wearing a little English jacket that made the peasants laugh. Sylvie alone thought me well dressed, but I did not dare to remind her of this opinion of so distant a time. I do not know why, but my mind went back to the wedding costumes we had put on at her aunt's cottage at Othys. I asked what had become of them.

"Ah! Dear aunt," Sylvie said, "she lent me the dress for the dance at Dammartin carnival two years ago. Poor aunt, the next year she died."

She sighed and wept so that I could not ask her how she happened to go to a fancy-dress ball; but I know that, thanks to her skill as a working woman, Sylvie was no longer a peasant girl. Her relations alone had remained in their original status, and she lived among them like an industrious fairy, shedding abundance about her.

XI

THE RETURN

The view widened as we left the wood. We had come to the bank of the Châalis lakes. The cloister galleries, the chapel with its pointed ogives, the feudal tower, and the little château that had sheltered the loves of Henry IV and Gabrielle were tinged with the evening glow against the dark green of the forest.

"It's a Walter Scott landscape," said Sylvie.

"And who has been telling you about Walter Scott?" I asked her. "You must have read a lot in the last three years!... Personally, I am trying to forget books, and what delights me is to see this old Abbey with you again, the ruins we used to hide in as little children. Do you remember, Sylvie, how frightened you were when the guardian told us the story of the red monks?"

"Oh, don't talk about it!"

"Well then, sing me the song of the fair maiden carried off from her father's garden, under the white rose tree."

"It's not sung any more."

"Have you become a musician?"

"A little."

"Sylvie, Sylvie, I am certain you sing opera arias!"

"And what's wrong with that?"

"Because I liked the old songs, and you won't know how to sing them any more."

Sylvie warbled a few notes from a grand aria out of a modern opera… She *phrased!*

We had strolled past the neighboring ponds and reached the green lawn, surrounded with limes and elms, where we had so often danced. I was conceited enough to point out the old Carolingian walls and to decipher the coats of arms of the House of Este.

"What about you?" Sylvie said. "How much more you've read than me! You're quite a savant, it seems."

I was irritated by her tone of reproach. Up to now I had been looking for a suitable place to renew our morning's moment of expansion; but what could I say to her, accompanied by a donkey and a very wide-awake small boy, who took a delight in coming up close to hear how a Parisian talked? Then I was unlucky enough to tell her about the apparition at Châalis, which had remained in my memory. I took Sylvie to the very hall of the château where I had heard Adrienne sing.

"Oh, do let me hear you!" I said to her. "Let your dear voice echo beneath these roofs and drive away the spirit that torments me, whether it be from heaven or from hell!"

She repeated the words and the song after me:

Angels of heaven, descend without delay
To the pit of purgatory!...

"It's very sad," she said.

"It's sublime... I think it's by Porpora,[15] with words translated in the sixteenth century."

"I don't know," Sylvie answered.

We went back by way of the valley, following the road to Charlepont, which the peasants, not very exact etymologists, called "Châllepont." Sylvie, tired of riding, leaned on my arm. The road was deserted; I tried to speak of what was in my heart, but somehow I could only find commonplace expressions, or else suddenly some pompous phrase from a novel — which Sylvie might have read. When we reached the walls of Saint-S*** we had to watch our steps. We went through marshy meadows with little winding streams.

"What has become of the nun?" I suddenly asked.

"You and your nun... Well, you see, that had an unhappy ending."

Sylvie would not tell me another word. Do women truly feel that such and such words come from the lips and not from the heart? One would scarcely think so, seeing that they are so easily deceived, and noticing the choice they most often make: there are some men who play the comedy of love so well! I could never do so, although I knew that some women knowingly allow themselves to be deceived. Besides, there is something sacred about a love that goes back to childhood... Sylvie, whom I had seen grow up, was as a sister to me. The thought of seducing her was impossible... Quite another idea came into my head. "At this moment," I said to myself, "I should be at the theater. What part is Aurélie" (for that was the actress's name) "playing this evening? Of course, the part of the princess in the new play. Ah, how moving she is in the third act... and in the love scene of the second! And with that wrinkled *jeune premier*..."

"Thinking again?" asked Sylvie, and she began singing:

> *At Dammartin are three fair maids,*
> *And one's as pretty as the day...*

"You little rogue," I cried, "you know perfectly well that you remember the old songs."

"If you came here more often, I would pick them up again," she said, "but we must be practical. You have your life in Paris, I have my work here; we mustn't be too late getting home: tomorrow morning I have to be up with the sun."

XII

PÈRE DODU

I was about to answer, I was about to fall at her feet, I was about to offer her my uncle's house, which I could still buy (there were several coheirs and the property had remained intact),[16] when at that moment we arrived at Loisy. Supper was waiting for us. The patriarchal smell of the onion soup was noticeable from a distance. Some neighbors had been invited for this day following the festival. I immediately recognized an old woodcutter, Père Dodu, who had told us such comic or terrible evening yarns in in the past. By turns shepherd, messenger, gamekeeper, fisherman, poacher even, Père

Dodu made cuckoo clocks and turnspits in his spare time. For some time now he had been consecrated as Ermenonville guide for English tourists, and he took them to Rousseau's places of meditation, relating the philosopher's last moments. He was the little boy whom Rousseau had employed to classify his plants for him and whom he had ordered to gather the stalks of hemlock from which he used to press the juice into his cup of coffee. The landlord of the Golden Cross disputed this detail with him — whence a prolonged feud. Père Dodu had for some time been in the possession of several entirely innocent secrets, such as how to cure a cow by saying a verse of the Bible backwards and making the sign of the cross with the left foot, but he had given up these superstitions in good time — thanks, he used to say, to his talks with Jean-Jacques.

"So there you are, little Parisian!" Père Dodu said to me. "Have you come to seduce our girls?"

"Me, Père Dodu?"

"You take them off into the woods while the wolf's away, don't you?"

"Père Dodu, you know you're the wolf."

"I used to be, as long as I could find sheep; at the moment I only meet goats, and they know how to defend themselves all right! But you Parisians, you're artful. Jean-Jacques was so right when he said, 'Man is corrupted in the poisoned atmosphere of cities.'"

"Père Dodu, you know very well that man is becoming corrupt everywhere."

Père Dodu began to sing a drinking song; it was in vain that they tried to stop him at a certain risky couplet (which everyone knew by heart). Sylvie refused to sing, in spite of our entreaties, saying that people no longer sang at table. I had already observed that the lover of the night before was seated at her left. There was something familiar in his round face and ruffled hair. He got up and came behind my chair, saying: "You don't remember me, Parisian?"

A good woman, who had just come in for dessert after having waited on us, said in my ear, "Don't you remember your foster brother?"

Without her warning I would have made a fool of myself.

"So it's you, Big Curly!" I said, "the fellow who pulled me out of the 'waater.' "

Sylvie burst out laughing at this recognition.

"Not to mention," he said, as he embraced me, "that you had a fine silver watch, and on the way back you were far more concerned about the watch than yourself, because it had stopped. You said, 'The brute's drownded, it won't go tic-tac, whatever will Uncle say?'..."

"A brute in a watch!" said Père Dodu. "So that's what they bring up children to believe in Paris!"

Sylvie was sleepy and I fancied I was completely lost in her esteem. She went upstairs to her room and as I kissed her, she said, "Come and see us tomorrow."

Père Dodu had remained at table with Sylvain[17] and my foster brother; we chatted for a long time over a flask of Louvres ratafia.

"All men are equal," declared Père Dodu in between two couplets. "I drink with a pastry cook as I would with a prince."

"Where's the pastry cook?" I asked.

"Look beside you — a young man ambitious to set himself up."

My foster brother seemed embarrassed. I understood it all. The fatality had been reserved for me to have a foster brother in a district made illustrious by Rousseau — who wanted to suppress wet nurses! Père Dodu informed me that there was much talk of a marriage between Sylvie and Big Curly, who wanted to set up a pastry business in Dammartin. I asked no more. Next day the coach from Nanteuil-le-Haudoin took me back to Paris.

XIII

AURÉLIE

To Paris! The coach took five hours. I was in no hurry to get there before the evening. Around eight o'clock I was in my usual stall; Aurélie lent her charm and inspiration to some verses feebly inspired by Schiller for which we were indebted to a talent of the time.[18] In the garden scene she was sublime. During the fourth act, when she did not come on, I went and bought a bouquet of flowers at Madame Prévost's. In it I placed a most tender letter signed "An Unknown." I said to myself, "That's something of the future settled." And the next day I was traveling to Germany.

What was I going to do there? Try and get my feelings into order. If I were writing a novel, I should never get anyone to believe in the story of a heart simultaneously smitten by two loves. Sylvie slipped from me through my own mistake; but the sight of her for a single day had sufficed to elevate my soul; henceforth I placed her like a smiling statue in the temple of Wisdom. Her gaze had held me back on the brink of an abyss. Still more vigorously I rejected the idea of presenting myself to Aurélie, to struggle with so many common lovers who scintillated for an instant by her side and then fell back broken. I said to myself: "Some day we shall see if the woman has a heart."

One morning I read in a newspaper that Aurélie was ill. I wrote to her from the mountains of Salzburg. My letter was so full of German mysticism that I could not expect much success from it, but then I did not ask for an answer. I counted somewhat on chance and on — *the unknown.*

Months passed. While I was traveling and idling, I had undertaken to put into poetic action the love of the painter Colonna for the fair Laura, whom her parents made a nun, and whom he loved until death. Something in the subject touched on my own constant preoccupation, and, the last line of the play written, I thought only of returning to France.[19]

What can I say now that is not the story of so many others? I passed through all the circles of those places of purgatory called theaters. "I ate the drum and drank the cymbal," to use the apparently meaningless phrase of the initiates of Eleusis. It doubtless means that when necessary we have to pass beyond the limits of nonsense and absurdity: for me, reason was conquering and holding my ideal.

Aurélie had accepted the principal part in the drama I brought back from Germany.[20] I shall never forget the day she allowed me to read the piece to her. The love scenes were written expressly for her. I believe I read them with spirit, but above all enthusiastically. In the conversation that followed I revealed myself as the *Unknown* of the two letters. She said to me, "You're quite crazy, but come and see me again... I have never met anyone who knew how to love me."

O woman! You are looking for love... what am I doing?

During the following days I wrote her what were doubtless the most tender and beautiful letters she had ever received. Her replies were full of good sense. One moment she was touched, called me to her, and admitted to me that it was very difficult for her to break off an earlier attachment.

"If it is really for me myself that you love me," she said, "you will understand that I can only belong to one man."

Two months later I received a gushing letter. I hurried to her. Meanwhile someone had given me a precious piece of information. The handsome young man I had met one night at the club had just joined the spahis.

Next summer there were races at Chantilly and the company to which Aurélie belonged gave a performance. Once in the country the players were for three days at the order of the manager. I had become friendly with this fellow, a former Dorante in the comedies of Marivaux, for a long time a *jeune premier* in drama, his last success having been the lover's part in the play imitated from Schiller in which my opera glasses had revealed him to me as so wrinkled. Off the stage he seemed younger, and as he was still slim he could still produce an effect in the provinces. He had fire. I went with the company in the capacity of "gentleman poet" and I persuaded the manager to give some performances at Senlis and Dammartin. He inclined at first to Compiègne, but Aurélie sided with me. Next day, while negotiations were going on with the owners of the halls and the local authorities, I hired some horses and we took the road to the ponds of Commelle to lunch at the castle of Queen Blanche. Aurélie, in riding habit and her fair hair loose, rode through the forest like a queen of old time, and the peasants stopped in amazement. Madame de F***[21] was the only lady they had ever seen so imposing and so graceful in her manner of greeting. After lunch we went down into the Swiss-like villages, where the waters of the Nonette work the sawmills. These scenes, so dear to my memory, interested Aurélie without arresting her. I had planned to take her to the château near Orry to the same square of green where for the first time I had seen Adrienne. She showed no emotion. Then I told her everything; I told her the origin of that love half-seen in my nights, then dreamed of, then realized in her. She listened to me seriously and told me: "It's not me you are in love with. You expect me to say, 'The actress is the same person as the nun.' You are simply seeking for drama, that's all, and the end eludes you. Go on, I don't believe in you any more."

These words were a flash of light. The strange enthusiasms I had felt for so long, the dreams, tears, despairs, and tenderness... weren't they then love? Then where is love?

That evening Aurélie played at Senlis. I thought I detected a weakness in her for the manager — the wrinkled *jeune premier.* The man had an excellent character and had done a great deal for her.

One day Aurélie told me: "There's the man who really loves me!"

XIV

LAST LEAVES

Such are the delusions which charm and beguile us in the morning of life. I have tried to set them down without too much order but many hearts will understand mine. Illusions fall, like the husks of a fruit, one after another, and what is left is experience. It has a bitter taste, but there is something tonic in its sharpness — forgive me this old-fashioned manner. Rousseau claims that the contemplation of nature is a balm for everything. Sometimes I try to find my woods of Clarens lost in the mists somewhere to the north of Paris.

All that has altered.

O Ermenonville, land where the old idylls lived, retranslated from Gessner, you have lost your lone star which shone for me with a double light. Now blue, now rose-colored, like the deceptive star of Aldebaran, it was Adrienne or Sylvie — two halves of a single love. One was the sublime ideal, the other the sweet reality. What are your lakes and shades to me now, what is your "Desert"? Othys, Montagny, Loisy, poor neighboring villages, Châalis (oh, that they would restore it), you have retained nothing of this past! Sometimes I need to revisit these scenes of solitude and reverie. In my own sad heart I find fugitive traces of a time when the natural was affected; sometimes I smile when I read on the side of granite memorials some verses of Roucher[22] which I once thought sublime — or benevolent maxims over a fountain or a grotto dedicated to Pan. The ponds, dug at such expense, are expanses of stagnant water disdained by the swans. No longer does the hunt of the Condé pass by with their noble women riders, no more do the horns answer each other from afar, multiplied by their echoes!... Today there is no direct road to Ermenonville. Sometimes I go there by Creil and Senlis, sometimes by Dammartin.

It is only in the evening that you reach Dammartin. I put up at an inn called the *Image of Saint John.* As a rule they give me quite a clean room, hung with old tapestry and a pier glass on the wall. This room is a last return to that bric-a-brac I long ago gave up. I sleep snugly under the eiderdown, customary in those parts. In the morning I open my window, framed in vines and roses, and discover with delight ten leagues of green horizon on which the poplars are aligned like armies. Here and there a few villages nestle under their steep spires, built, as they put it here, like pointed bones. First there is Othys — then Ève, then Ver; Ermenonville would be visible through the woods if only it had a spire, but in that philosophic spot the church has been neglected. I fill my lungs with the pure air from the plain and go down in good spirits to pay a visit to the pastry shop.

"So there you are, Big Curly!"

"Hallo, little Parisian!"

We exchange a few affectionate punches of childhood, then I climb a certain staircase where my arrival is greeted by the happy cries of two children. Sylvie's Athenian smile lights her lovely features. I say to myself, "Perhaps this is happiness; and yet..."

Sometimes I call her Lolotte and she finds a certain resemblance in me to Werther, less the pistols, which are out of fashion these days. While Big Curly prepares breakfast, we take the children for a walk in the avenues of lime trees which encircle the ruins of the old brick towers of the château. While the little ones amuse themselves by shooting a few arrows from their father's bow into the target on the shooting-ground of the Companions of the Bow, we read a little poetry or a few pages from those short books that are scarcely ever written now.

I forgot to say that on the day when Aurélie's company gave a performance at Dammartin, I took Sylvie to see it and asked her if she did not think the actress like someone she knew.

"Who do you mean?"

"Do you remember Adrienne?"

She burst out laughing and said, "What an idea!" Then, as if reproving herself, she sighed and added, "Poor Adrienne! She died in the convent of Saint-S***... about 1832."

OCTAVIE

In the spring of 1835 I was seized by an intense desire to see Italy. Each day I awoke already inhaling the pungent scent of alpine chestnut trees; in the evening, Terni's waterfall, the frothing source of the Tevere, gushed forth for me alone from the scratched framework of a small theater's flats... A charming voice, like that of the sirens, murmured in my ears, as if the reeds of the Trasimeno had suddenly taken on a voice... I needed to set out, to leave in Paris a frustrated love which I hoped to escape through distraction.

My first stop was Marseilles. Every morning, I swam in the sea at the Château Vert, glimpsing in the distance the cheery islands of the gulf. I met an English girl in this azure bay, whose slender body would cleave the green water next to me. This daughter of the waters, whose name was Octavie, one day came to me glorying in a strange catch she had made. In her white hands she held a fish which she gave to me.

I couldn't help smiling at such a gift. Meanwhile, cholera was reigning over the city, and to avoid the quarantines, I decided to travel by land. I saw Nice, Genoa and Florence; I marveled at the Cathedral and the Baptistery, the masterpieces of Michelangelo, the leaning tower and the Camposanto of Pisa. Then, taking the Spoleto route, I stopped for ten days in Rome. Saint Peter's Cathedral, the Vatican, the Coliseum: all seemed to me like a dream. I hastened to catch the post for Civita Vecchia, where I had to embark. — For three days the raging sea delayed the steamer's arrival. I walked pensively along the desolate beach, where I was very nearly devoured one day by dogs.

— The day before I left, a theater was performing a French vaudeville. A vivacious, blond woman caught my eye. It was the English girl, seated in a loge up front. She was accompanying her father, who appeared to be infirm; he had been advised by doctors to seek out the climate of Naples.

The next morning I paid for my passage in high spirits. The English girl was on the deck, pacing back and forth with long strides and, impatient with the slowness of the ship, she pressed her ivory teeth into the peel of a lemon.

"Poor girl," I said, "your chest is ailing you, I'm sure of it, and it's a pity."

She stared at me: "Who told you that?"

"The sibyl of Tibur," I told her without changing my expression.

"Go on," she said, "I don't believe a word of it."

So saying, she looked at me tenderly and I couldn't help kissing her hand.

"If I were stronger," she said, "I'd teach you to lie!…" And laughing, she threatened me with a golden-headed switch that she was holding in her hand.

Our ship was nearing the port of Naples and we were crossing the bay between Ischia and Nisida, which were flooded with the fiery glow of the Orient. "If you love me," she continued, "you will wait for me tomorrow at Portici. I don't make such appointments with everyone."

She disembarked and accompanied her father to the Hotel di Roma, which had recently been built along the pier. As for me, I went to find some lodging behind the Florentine Theater. I spent the day wandering all over the Via Toledo and the harbor, and visiting the Museum; that evening I went to see the ballet at the San Carlo. There I chanced to meet the Marquis Gargallo, whom I had known in Paris, and who took me after the show to have tea at his sisters'.

I will never forget the delightful soirée that followed. The marchioness did the honors and showed me around an immense salon filled with strangers. The conversation was a little like that of the Précieuses; I felt as if I were in the blue room of the Hôtel Rambouillet. I discerned the glory of ancient Greece in the sisters of the marquis, who were as lovely as the Graces. They discussed the shape of the Eleusinian stone, debating at length as to whether its form was triangular or square. The marchioness would have assuredly been able to settle the matter, for she was as beautiful and noble as Vesta herself. I left the palace, my head dizzy from this philosophical discussion, and was unable to find my accommodations. Wandering through the city, I was bound to become the hero of some affair. The encounter I had that night is the subject of the following letter, which I later sent to her, the fatal love I believed I had escaped in distancing myself from Paris.

I am extremely apprehensive. I haven't seen you in four days or at least I haven't seen you alone; I have an ominous feeling. I believe you have been sincere with me; whether you have changed in these last few days, I don't know, but I fear it. My God! Take pity on my suspicions, or you'll surely bring down some calamity upon us. Even so, I would hold myself responsible. I displayed more timidity and devotion than a man ever should. I restrained myself to such an extent, I was so afraid of offending you, you who had already punished me once before, that perhaps I was overly tactful, allowing you to believe my passion had cooled. Well, I honored a day important to you, I suppressed emotions strong enough to crush my soul, and I donned a cheerful mask, I, whose heart was constricted and on fire. No one else will ever have so much regard for your feelings, but then perhaps, no one has shown you such true affection, and felt so deeply your true worth.

Let's speak frankly. I know there are ties a woman can only sever with difficulty, awk-

ward relationships that must be broken off slowly. Are the sacrifices I've asked of you too great? If they are a source of irritation, tell me, I will understand. Neither your fears, your whims, nor your social duties can weaken the deep affection I have for you, nor cloud the purity of my love. Together we will see what we can accept and what we cannot, and if there are ties that must be severed and not merely undone, depend on me to take care of them. To lack candor now would be cruel, for as I have told you, my life is at your command, and you know that my greatest desire can only be to die for you!

To die, good heavens! Why does this notion constantly recur to me, as if my death were the only equivalent of the bliss you make me hope for? Death! This word, however, casts no shadow over my thoughts. I see her wreathed in pale roses, as if at the end of a feast; I sometimes dream of her waiting for me, smiling, at the bedside of an adored woman, after the joy, after the ecstasy, saying: "Let's go, young man! You have had your share of happiness in this world. Now come sleep, come rest in my arms. I may not be beautiful, but I am kindhearted and benevolent; I may not give pleasure, but I provide everlasting peace."

But where have I seen this image before? Ah! That's right, it was in Naples, three years ago. One night, near the Villa Reale, I met a young woman who resembled you, a very good creature whose occupation was embroidering church ornaments in gold. She seemed lost in thought; I escorted her home, even though she had a lover in the Swiss guard who she feared might show up. She had no difficulty, however, in confessing that she preferred me... What can I say? I took it into my head to forget my sorrow for an evening, and imagined that this woman, whose language I scarcely understood, was you, come to me by magic. Why conceal this affair and the strange illusion that my heart accepted so easily, especially after the several glasses of sparkling Lacrima Christi poured for me at supper? The room I entered had something mystical about it, either by chance or through the remarkable choice of objects that it contained. A black Madonna covered in rags, whose antique costume my hostess was to restore, stood upon a chest of drawers by a bed draped with green serge; further off, a figure of Saint Rosalie, wreathed in violet roses, seemed to be guarding the crib of a sleeping child; the walls were whitewashed and decorated with paintings of the four elements representing mythological deities. In addition to all this, there was a considerable disarray of sparkling fabrics, artificial flowers, Etruscan vases, mirrors framed in a foil that reflected brilliantly the glow of a copper lamp, and on a table, a Tract on Divination and Dreams, leading me to think my companion was a bit of a sorceress, or at least a gypsy.

A pleasant old woman with great, solemn features went out, came in, serving us; I think it must have been her mother! And I, pensive, not saying a word, I just looked at her, this woman who reminded me so strongly of you.

She kept asking me: "Are you unhappy?" And I said to her: "Don't speak, I can hardly understand you; listening to and pronouncing Italian fatigues me." — "Oh!" she said, "I can speak differently." And suddenly she began to speak in a language I had never heard before. It was a mixture of sonorous syllables, gutturals, warblings full of charm, no doubt an ancient tongue: Hebrew, Syriac, I don't know. She smiled at my amazement and went to the chest of drawers from which she pulled baubles embedded with fake gems, necklaces, bangles, a crown; adorning herself with all this, she returned to the table and remained solemn for a long time. The old woman reentered the room and burst out laughing, telling me, I believe, that this was how she looked on holidays. Just then, the child woke up and began to cry. The two women rushed to its crib and soon the younger one returned, proudly holding in her arms the now pacified bambino.

She spoke to the child in this marvelous language, keeping him occupied with graceful coquetries; and I, little accustomed to the burnt wines of Vesuvius, felt the objects spinning before my eyes. This strange-mannered woman, royally adorned, proud and capricious, seemed to me like one of those magicians of Thessaly to whom one gave one's soul for a dream. Oh! Why do I not fear telling you this story? It is because you know this was only a dream, in which you alone reigned!

I tore myself from this phantom who both charmed and frightened me; I wandered through the deserted city until I heard the sound of the first bells; then, relishing the morning, I took to the side streets behind Chiaia, and started to climb the Posilipo above the grotto. I reached the top and walked around, gazing at the already blue sea, the city still absorbed in its morning sounds, and the islands of the bay, where the sun was beginning to gild the rooftops. I was not in the least saddened; I walked with great strides, I ran, I descended the slopes, I rolled in the damp grass; but in my heart there was the presence of death.

O God! What profound sadness dwelled in my heart, but it was only the cruel thought that I was not loved. I had seen in effect a phantom of happiness, I had made use of all of God's gifts, I was beneath the most beautiful sky in the world, in the presence of Nature at its most perfect, the most immense spectacle that is given man to see; but I was four hundred leagues from the woman I lived for, and who ignored my very existence. To be unloved and to lack even the hope of ever being so! It was then that I attempted to ask God the explanation for my singular existence. I had only to take a step — at the spot where I stood, the mountain was cut like a cliff, the sea rumbled below, blue and pure: no more than an instant in which to suffer. Oh! The intoxication of this thought was terrible. Twice I leapt, and I don't know what power threw me back alive upon the ground, which I clutched. No, my God! You did not create me for my eternal suffering. I do not want to offend you with my death; but give me the strength, give me the capacity, above all give me the determination that enables some to attain a throne, others glory, others love!

A rather unusual phenomenon occurred during this strange night. Just before dawn, all the doors and windows of the house I was in lit up, and a hot and sulphurous dust made it difficult to breath. Leaving my easy conquest asleep on the terrace, I entered the alleyways that lead to the Saint Elmo castle; — as I climbed the mountain, the pure morning air filled my lungs; it felt delightful to rest under the trellises of the villas, and I gazed without terror upon Vesuvius, still covered with a dome of smoke.

It was at this moment that I was seized by the intoxication of which I spoke; the thought of the rendezvous with the English girl tore me from the deadly ideas I had considered. After freshening my mouth with one of those enormous bunches of grapes the market women sell, I made my way towards Portici and went to visit the ruins of Herculaneum. The streets were dusted with a metallic ash. Near the ruins, I entered the subterranean city and for a long time walked from building to building, seeking from these monuments the secrets of their past. The temples of Venus, of Mercury, spoke to my imagination in vain. They needed to be inhabited by living figures. — I climbed back up to Portici and waited pensively beneath a trellis for my unknown woman.

She soon appeared, guiding her father who was walking with difficulty, and shook my hand with vigor, saying: "Very good." We chose a carriage and went to tour Pompeii. What a joy it was to guide her through the silent streets of that ancient Roman colony. I had studied the most secret passageways. When we reached the small temple of Isis, I had the pleasure of devotedly explaining the details of the worship and ceremonies I had read of in Apuleius. She wanted to reenact the character of the goddess, and I found myself in the role of Osiris, whose divine mysteries I then described.

As we were coming back, I was struck by the grandeur of the ideas we had stirred up, and did not dare speak to her of love... She found me so cold that she reproached me. I then confessed I no longer felt worthy of her. I recounted the mystery of the apparition which had awakened an old love in my heart, and told her of all the sadness that followed this fatal night; a night in which the phantom of happiness had become only the reproach of a betrayal.

Alas! How distant that all is! Ten years ago, I passed through Naples again, returning from the Orient. I went down to the Hotel di Roma, and there found the English girl. She had married a famous painter who, shortly after their marriage, was overcome by a complete paralysis; lying upon a couch, nothing moved in his face save for two large, black eyes. He was still young and unable to even hope for a recovery which another climate might offer. The poor woman had devoted her life to living sadly with her husband and her father, and her gentleness, her absolute lack of guile could not manage to calm the atrocious jealousy that smoldered in the heart of the former. Nothing could ever persuade him to let his wife leave his side. He reminded me of that black giant staying eternally awake in the cave of the spirits, who to avoid falling asleep forces his wife to beat him. O mystery of the human soul! One must see in such a tableau the cruel marks of the gods' vengeance!

I could not take more than a day of this misery. The ship that brought me back to Marseilles carried away like a dream the memory of this beloved apparition; and I think now that perhaps I left my happiness there. Octavie has kept this secret to herself.

ISIS

Before the railroad from Naples to Resina was built, a trip to Pompeii was quite a journey. One needed a day to successively visit Herculaneum, Vesuvius — and Pompeii, located two miles further. It was common practice to remain there until the following day in order to roam through the ruins by the moonlight, and thus fall prey to a complete illusion. One could actually imagine that, traveling back over the course of centuries, it was suddenly possible to wander through the streets and squares of the sleeping city; the peaceful moon was perhaps more suitable than the bright sun for these ruins, which at first provoke neither admiration nor surprise, and whose antiquity displays itself, so to speak, in a modest state of undress.

A few years ago, one of the ambassadors residing in Naples gave a rather ingenious party. — He had a great number of people dress up in the style of the ancients; the guests complied and for a day and a night, they practiced the various customs of the ancient Roman colony. Erudition had determined most of the party's details; chariots traveled up and down the streets, tradesmen filled the shops; at certain hours, the different parties of guests gathered together in the main houses for a light meal. Pansa, the town councillor, was there, as was Sallust, and Julia Felix, the opulent daughter of Scaurus,[1] all welcoming the guests and receiving them into their homes. — The women in the House of the Vestals were veiled, but those in the House of the Dancers were less deceitful as to the promises of their gracious attributes. The two theaters offered performances both comic and tragic. Under the colonnades of the Forum idle citizens exchanged the news of the day, while from the open basilica, the sharp voices of advocates and the imprecations of litigants rang out into the square. — Cloth and hangings completed the decoration wherever these scenes took place, with which the general lack of roofing would have conflicted; but apart from this detail, the preservation of most of the buildings is complete enough for one to have taken great pleasure from this palingenetic endeavor. — One of the most curious scenes was the ceremony performed at sunset in that admirable little temple of Isis, which, due to its complete preservation, is perhaps the most interesting of all these ruins.

This party gave rise to the following research, concerning the conventions which affected the Egyptian cult when it came to struggle directly with the nascent religion of Christ.

As powerful and appealing as this revived cult of Isis was for the enervated men of this period, it acted primarily upon the women. — The strange ceremonies and mysteries of the Cabiri, the Eleusinian and Greek gods, and the Bacchanalia of *Liber Pater* and *Hebon* of Campania: all helped feed a passion for the supernatural and even for superstition. All this was absorbed, through religious artifice, into the Egyptian goddess's secret cult, as if into a subterranean canal which receives the water from a confluence of tributaries.

In addition to the monthly holidays and celebrations, there was a public assembly and service twice a day for believers of both sexes. The goddess was up and about at the very first hour of the day, and those who required her particular blessing came for morning prayer when she got up. — The temple was opened with great pomp. The high priest came out from the sanctuary accompanied by his ministers. Scented incense was smoking on the altar; the gentle sounds of a flute could be heard. — The community had meanwhile divided itself into two rows, from the vestibule all the way up to the first step of the temple. — The priest's voice begins the prayer, a sort of litany is chanted; then the sistrum of Isis rings out loudly from the hands of some worshipers. A part of the goddess's history is often portrayed by means of pantomime and symbolic dances. The basic principles of her cult are invoked for the kneeling people, who sing or murmur all sorts of orisons.

But if they had celebrated the matins of the goddess at sunrise, they could not neglect to offer her their evening salutations as well, and to wish her a happy night, a particular formula which constituted one of the important parts of the liturgy. They began by announcing to the goddess herself the *evening's hour.*

The ancients, it is true, did not have the convenience of chiming clocks, nor even silent clocks; but they compensated, as much as they could, for our steel and copper machines with living machines: slaves in charge of crying out the hour which they read from the clepsydra and the sundial; — there were even men who, from just the length of their shadows, which they could estimate at a quick glance, were able to tell the exact hour of the day or evening. — This custom of crying out the measurements of time was practiced in the temples as well. In Rome there were devout people who performed for Jupiter Capitolinus this singular duty of telling him the time. — But this custom was observed principally at the matins and vespers of the great Isis, and it was on this that the organization of the daily liturgy depended.

II

This was done in the afternoon, at the ceremonious closing of the temple, around 4 o'clock according to the modern division of time, or, according to the ancient division, after the eighth hour of the day. — One could literally call it the going-to-bed ceremony of the goddess. From time immemorial, the gods have endured by conforming to the customs and habits of men. — On Mount Olympus, Homer's *Zeus* leads a patriarchal existence with his wives, his sons and his daughters, living in every respect like Priam and Arsinoüs[2] in the Trojan and Phoenician lands. Since the two great divinities of the Nile, Isis and Serapis, were settling in Rome and on the shores of Italy, it was just as necessary that they adapted themselves to the Roman's way of life. — One arose early in Rome, even in the time of the last emperors; by the first or second hour of the day, everything was active on the squares, in the courts of justice and in the markets. — But later on, by the eighth hour of the day, or four in the afternoon, all activity had stopped. Isis was then glorified again in a ceremonious evening prayer.

The other parts of the liturgy were mostly those performed at the matins. The difference, however, was that the litanies and hymns were sung to the sound of sistrums, flutes and trumpets, by a psalmist or precentor, who in the priests' order fulfilled the functions of hymnodist. — At the most solemn moment, the high priest, standing upon the top step, before the tabernacle, flanked by two deacons or pastophorus, lifted up the principal element of the cult, the symbol of the fertile Nile, *the holy water,* and displayed it to the fervent adoration of the congregation. The ceremony ended with the usual leave-taking.

The superstitions attached to certain days, the ablutions, the fastings, the expiations, the mortifications and scourgings of the flesh, were the prelude to the consecration to the most saintly goddess of a thousand qualities and virtues with which men and women, after so many trials and sacrifices, elevated themselves through the three levels. One's introduction to these mysteries, however, opened the door to some excesses. — These preparations and trials, which no husband dared refuse his wife, no lover dared refuse his mistress, for fear of Osiris's whip or Isis's vipers, often lasted a great number of days. Dubious rendezvous were arranged in the sanctuaries, covered in the dark veils of initiation. — But these are excesses common to all cults in their periods of decadence. The same accusations could be addressed to the mysterious practices and banquets of the first Christians. — The idea of a *Holy Land* joining together for all nations the recollection of early traditions and a sort of filial adoration — of a holy water suitable for the consecrations and purifications of believers — this is what provides nobler similarities to examine between these two cults, of which the first served, so to speak, as a transition to the other.

All water was sweet to the Egyptian, but particularly that which had been drawn from the river, the emanation of Osiris. — At the annual holiday of the rediscovered Osiris, after lengthy lamentations, everybody cried out: "We have found him and we rejoice!" and threw themselves to the ground before the high priest who was carrying the pitcher filled with the newly drawn water of the Nile; they lifted their hands to the sky, praising the miracle of divine mercy.

This holy water, kept in a sacred pitcher, also played a part in the holiday of Isis, being the most compelling symbol of the father of the living and the dead. Isis could not be honored without Osiris. — The faithful even believed that Osiris was actually present in the water of the Nile. At each evening and morning benediction, the high priest displayed to the people the *hydria*, the sacred pitcher, and offered it for their adoration. — Nothing was overlooked in the effort to deeply impress the nature of this divine transubstantiation upon the audience's spirit. — The prophet himself, as great as the saintliness of this personage was, could not grasp with his bare hands this vase which held the divine mystery. — On a stole of the finest cloth, he wore a sort of cape *(piviale)*, of either linen or muslin, covering his shoulders and arms, with which he wrapped up his arm and hand. — In this way, he picked up the holy vase, which he then carried, according to Saint Clement of Alexandria, tightly against his chest. — Besides, what virtue did the Nile not possess in the eyes of the pious Egyptian? It was spoken of everywhere as a source of healing and miracles. — There were vases in which its water was preserved for years. "I have in my cellar some water of the Nile that is four years old," said the Egyptian merchant with pride to the resident of Byzantium or Naples who vaunted his aged Falernian or Chian wine. Even after his death, under his wrappings and in his mummified condition, the Egyptian hoped that Osiris would still allow him to quench his thirst with his venerated waters. "Osiris gives you cool water!" read the epitaphs of the dead. It is for this reason mummies wear a painted goblet upon their chest.

III

Perhaps by reading too much beforehand, one risks spoiling one's first impression of celebrated places. I had visited the Orient with nothing but the memories, already hazy, of my classical education. — Returning from Egypt, Naples was to me a place of rest and study, and the precious depositories of its libraries and museums aided me in justifying or combating the surmises that my mind had formed at the sight of so many inexplicable and silent ruins. — Perhaps it was to my vivid memory of Alexandria, Thebes and the Pyramids that I owed the almost religious emotion I felt upon my second viewing of the temple of Isis in Pompeii. I had left my fellow travelers as they marveled at the house of Diomedes in all its details, and, slipping away from the attendants, plunged aimlessly into the streets of the ancient city, avoiding here and there some invalid who asked me from a distance where I was going. I worried little about knowing the name that science had uncovered for such-and-such edifice, temple, house, or shop. Was it not enough that the dragomen and Arabs had spoiled the pyramids for me, without having to be subjected to the Neapolitan *ciceroni?* I had entered through the street of the tombs, following this road paved with lava, in which the deep ruts of the ancient wheels were still visible. I knew that I would find the Egyptian goddess's temple again at the city's limit, next to the theater of tragedy. I recognized the narrow courtyard once enclosed by a gate, the still-standing columns, the two altars on the right and left, the latter of which is perfectly preserved, and at the far end the ancient *cella* rising on seven steps, surfaced in bygone days with marble from Paros.

Eight columns of the Doric order, without the base, support the sides, and ten others the pediment; the surrounding enclosure is exposed, in accordance with the genre of architecture known as *hypætron*,[3] but a covered portico stood over it. The sanctuary is a small, square, vaulted temple covered in tiles, and presents three niches intended for the pictures of the Egyptian Trinity;

— two altars located at the far end of the sanctuary bore the Isiac tablets, one of which was still preserved, and on the base of the main statue of the goddess, set in the center of the inner nave, one can read that *L. C. Phœbus* erected it on this spot by decree of the decurions.

Near the altar on the left, in the courtyard, was a small lodge intended for purifications; some bas-reliefs decorated its walls. Two vases holding lustral water were set at the entrance of the inner doorway, in the manner of our stoups. Stucco paintings decorated the interior of the temple and depicted country scenes, plants and animals of Egypt — the sacred land.

At the museum I had admired the treasures that were removed from this temple: the lamps, the goblets, the censers, the cruets, the aspergilla, the miters and sparkling crosiers of the priests, the sistrums, the bugles and cymbals, a gilded Venus, a Bacchus, some Hermes, seats of silver and ivory, idols of basalt and mosaic paving stones embellished with inscriptions and emblems. The precious material and craftsmanship of these objects are an indication of the temple's sumptuousness. The majority of them were found in the most removed holy place, behind the sanctuary, which one reaches by passing through five archways. There, a small oblong courtyard leads to a room which once held sacred ornaments. The residence of the Isiac ministers, located to the left of the temple, consisted of three rooms, in which several corpses of these priests had been found. One must assume that their religion made it a duty to not abandon the sanctuary.

This temple is the best preserved ruin of Pompeii, for at the time in which the city was buried, it was the newest building. The ancient temple had been knocked down a few years previously by an earthquake, and what we have now is what was rebuilt in its place. — I do not know if any of the three statues of Isis in the Naples museum was found on this same spot, but I had admired them the day before, and joining to them the recollection of the two paintings, nothing prevented me from reconstructing in my mind the whole scene of the evening ceremony.

The sun was, in fact, beginning to go down towards Capri, and the moon was slowly rising up the side of Vesuvius, which was covered with a light canopy of smoke. — I sat down upon a stone, gazing at these two stars that had been adored for so long in this temple under the names of Osiris and Isis, and under the mystical attributes relating to their various phases. I felt overwhelmed by an intense emotion. Child of a century more sceptical than unbelieving, vacillating between two opposite upbringings — that of the Revolution, which repudiated everything, and that of social reaction, which claims to restore the whole of Christian beliefs — would I find myself led to believe everything, as our fathers the philosophers had been led to deny everything? — I was musing over that magnificent preamble to Volney's *Ruins*, in which the spirit of the past appears on the ruins of Palmyra, borrowing from such lofty inspirations only the power to destroy, piece by piece, all the religious traditions of the human race! In this manner, Christ himself perished through the efforts of modern reason; Christ, the last of the enlighteners, who in bygone days had depopulated the heavens in the name of a higher reason. O Nature! O Eternal Mother! Was that truly the fate reserved for the last of your celestial sons? Have mortals come to reject all hope and prestige? When the most daring of your followers raised your sacred veil, goddess of Saïs, did he then find himself face to face with the image of Death?

If the successive collapse of beliefs led to this result, would it not be more comforting to go to the opposite extreme and try to recover the illusions of the past?

IV

It is evident that in its final days paganism had reimmersed itself in its Egyptian origins, and aimed more and more at restoring the diverse mythological conceptions to the principle of unity. This eternal Nature, which Lucretius the materialist invoked under the name of celestial Venus, was by preference named Cybele by Julian, and Urania or Ceres by Plotinus, Proclus and Porphyry; — Apuleius, while allowing her all these names, is more willing to call her Isis; it is the name which, for him, sums up all the others; it is the original identity of this queen of heaven, of diverse attributes, of the changing mask! She also appears to him in Egyptian dress, but freed from the stiff bearing, the strips of cloth and the naïve forms of early times.

Her long, thick locks of hair flow over her divine shoulders; a multiform and multifloral wreath adorns her head, and the silvery moon shines upon her brow; snakes wind through both sides of her blond tufts of hair, and the changing reflections of her dress pass, in accordance with the movement of its folds, from the purest white to a saffron yellow, or seem to take on the redness of the flame; her dark black coat is spangled with stars and trimmed with a luminous fringe; her right hand holds the sistrum, which produces a clear sound, her left hand a golden vase in the form of a gondola.

Thus she appeared to Lucius, exhaling the most delicious perfumes of Arabia, and said to him: "I have been moved by your prayers; I, the mother of nature, mistress of the elements, the original source of the centuries, the greatest of divinities, queen of the manes; I, in whom the gods and goddesses merge; I, the unique and almighty divinity worshiped by the universe under a thousand forms. Thus I am named Cybele in Phrygia; in Athens, Minerva; in Cyprus, Paphian Venus; in Crete, Dictynne Diana; in Sicily, Stygian Persephone; in Eleusis, the ancient Ceres; elsewhere, Juno, Bellona, Hecate or Nemesis, whereas the Egyptians, whose learning preceded all other nations, pay me homage under my true name, the goddess Isis.

"Bear in mind," she said to Lucius after showing him the means of escaping the spell which held him victim, "that you must devote the rest of your life to me, and even when you have crossed the dark shore you will continue to worship me, be it in the gloom of Acheron or in the Elysian Fields; and if, through the observation of my cult and through an inviolable chastity, you are worthy of me, you will discover that I alone can prolong your spiritual life beyond the marked limits." — Having uttered these lovely words, the invincible goddess vanished and gathered herself *into her own immensity.*

Of course, if paganism had always demonstrated such a pure conception of the divinity, the religious principles stemming from the old world of Egypt would still reign over modern civilization. — But is it not remarkable that the early foundations of the Christian faith also came from Egypt? Orpheus and Moses, both initiated to the Isiac mysteries, simply announced to various races some sublime truths — then altered little by little, if not transformed completely, by the difference in customs, languages and the span of time. — Today, it seems that Catholicism itself has undergone, depending on the country, a reaction analogous to that which had taken place in the last years of polytheism. In Italy, in Poland, Greece, Spain, among all peoples most genuinely attached to the Roman church, has not the religious devotion to the Virgin become something of an exclusive cult? Is it not still the Holy Mother, holding in her arms the child savior and mediator who rules over the spirits — and whose apparition still brings about conversions comparable to that of Apuleius's hero? It is not only by the child in her arms or the cross in her hand that Isis resembles the Virgin: the same sign of the zodiac is consecrated to them, the moon is under their feet; the same nimbus shines about their heads; we have mentioned above many analogous details in their ceremonies; — the same sentiment of chastity in the Isiac cult, in so far as its doctrine remained pure; similar institutions of societies and brotherhoods. I will certainly take care not to draw from all these parallels the same conclusions as Volney and Dupuis. On the contrary, to the eyes of the philosopher, if not the theologian — does it not seem that there was some degree of divine revelation in all these intelligent cults? Early Christianity invoked the word of the sibyls and did not reject the testimony of the last of the Delphic oracles. A new evolution of dogma could make all the different religious testimonies agree on certain points. It would be so lovely to absolve and rescue the heroes and sages of antiquity from their eternal maledictions!

Far be it from me, of course, to have gathered together the preceding details only to prove that the Christian religion made numerous borrowings from the last formulas of paganism: no one denies this point. Any religion which succeeds another respects for a long time certain practices and forms of the cult, which it merely harmonizes with its own dogma. In this way the Greeks modified and translated the ancient theogony of the Egyptians and Pelasgians, adorning it with new names and attributes; — later still, in the religious stage which we have just depicted, Serapis, who was already a transformation of Osiris, evolved into Jupiter; Isis, who to enter into Greek myth had only to resume her name of Io, daughter of Inachus — the founder of the Eleusinian mysteries — rejected henceforth the bestial mask, symbol of an era of struggle and servitude. But look at how many easy assimilations Christianity had found in these rapid transformations of the most diverse dogmas! — Let us leave aside Serapis's *cross* and the dwelling place in the underworld of this god *who judges souls;* — the *Redeemer* promised to the world, whom the poets and oracles had long anticipated, is it the child Horus nursed by the divine mother, and who will be the *Word* (logos) of future ages? — is it Iacchus-Iesus of the Eleusinian mysteries, already older and soaring from the arms of Demeter, the *pantheistic* goddess? Or rather, is it not true that one must reunite all these diverse forms of the same idea, and that it was always an admirable theogonic thought to present to mankind's adoration a Heavenly Mother whose child is the hope of the world?

And now, why these rapturous cries of joy, these songs of heaven, these palm leaves that are being waved, these sacred cakes that are shared on certain days of the year? It is because the child savior was once born at this same time. — Why these other days of tears and lugubrious songs in which one seeks the body of a bruised and bleeding god — in which moanings echo from the banks of the Nile to the shores of Phoenicia, from the heights of Lebanon to the plains where Troy once stood? Why is the one that is sought and mourned for here called Osiris, elsewhere Adonis, and elsewhere Atys? And why does another clamor coming from the far end of Asia also seek in the mysterious grottos the remains of an immolated god? — A deified woman, mother, wife, or lover, bathes with her tears this bleeding and disfigured body, this victim of a hostile principle which triumphs through his death, but which one day will be vanquished! The celestial victim is presented in marble or wax, with his flesh tones stained in blood, with his running wounds which the faithful come to piously touch and kiss. But on the third day everything changes: the body gone, the immortal is revealed; joy follows the tears, hope is reborn in the world; it is the renewed holiday of youth and spring.

That, then, is the Eastern cult, both primitive and subsequent to the Greek fables, and which had ended by overcoming and absorbing bit by bit the domain of Homer's gods. The mythological sky shone forth with too pure a brilliance, it was of too precise and too clear a beauty, it radiated too much happiness, abundance and serenity, it was, in a word, too well conceived from the viewpoint of happy people, of rich and victorious nations, to impose itself for long on a troubled and suffering world. — It had triumphed through the Greeks and their victory in that almost cosmogonic struggle of which Homer sang, and from then on the strength and glory of the gods was embodied in the destinies of Rome; — but grief and the desire for revenge influenced the rest of the world, which no longer wanted anything but religions of despair. — Philosophy, moreover, managed to take on the work of assimilation and moral unity; what was expected from the spirits was realized in the order of facts. This divine Mother, this Savior, that a kind of prophetic mirage had heralded from one end of the world to the other, finally appeared like the broad daylight which follows the vague glow of the dawn.

LES CHIMÈRES/THE CHIMERAS

EL DESDICHADO

Je suis le ténébreux, — le veuf, — l'inconsolé,
Le prince d'Aquitaine à la tour abolie:
Ma seule *étoile* est morte, — et mon luth constellé
Porte le *Soleil noir* de la *Mélancolie.*

Dans la nuit du tombeau, toi qui m'as consolé,
Rends-moi le Pausilippe et la mer d'Italie,
La *fleur* qui plaisait tant à mon cœur désolé,
Et la treille où le pampre à la rose s'allie.

Suis-je Amour ou Phébus?... Lusignan ou Biron?
Mon front est rouge encor du baiser de la reine;
J'ai rêvé dans la grotte où nage la syrène...

Et j'ai deux fois vainqueur traversé l'Achéron:
Modulant tour à tour sur la lyre d'Orphée
Les soupirs de la sainte et les cris de la fée.

EL DESDICHADO (THE DISINHERITED)

I am the dark one, — the widower, — the unconsoled,
The prince of Aquitaine at his stricken tower:
My sole *star* is dead, — and my constellated lute
Bears the black *sun* of the *Melencolia.*

In the night of the tomb, you who consoled me,
Give me back Mount Posilipo and the Italian sea,
The *flower* which pleased so my desolate heart,
And the trellis where the grape vine unites with the rose.

Am I Amor or Phoebus?... Lusignan or Biron?
My forehead is still red from the kiss of the queen;
I have dreamd in the grotto where the mermaid swims...

And two times victorious I have crosst the Acheron:
Modulating turn by turn on the lyre of Orpheus
The sighs of the saint and the cries of the fay.

MYRTHO

Je pense à toi, Myrtho, divine enchanteresse,
Au Pausilippe altier, de mille feux brillant,
À ton front inondé des clartés d'Orient,
Aux raisins noirs mêlés avec l'or de ta tresse.

C'est dans ta coupe aussi que j'avais bu l'ivresse,
Et dans l'éclair furtif de ton œil souriant,
Quand aux pieds d'Iacchus on me voyait priant,
Car la Muse m'a fait l'un des fils de la Grèce.

Je sais pourquoi là-bas le volcan s'est rouvert...
C'est qu'hier tu l'avais touché d'un pied agile,
Et de cendres soudain l'horizon s'est couvert.

Depuis qu'un duc normand brisa tes dieux d'argile,
Toujours, sous les rameaux du laurier de Virgile,
Le pâle Hortensia s'unit au Myrthe vert!

MYRTHO

I think of thee, Myrtho, divine enchantress,
Of lofty Posilipo with a thousand fires glittering,
Of thy forehead flooded with lights of the Orient,
Of the black grapes mingled with the gold of your hair.

It is in your cup too that I used to drink drunkenness,
And in the furtive lightning of your eye smiling
When I was seen praying at the feet of Iacchus,
For the Muse had made me one of the sons of Greece.

I know why the volcano has reopend over there...
It's because you toucht it yesterday with a light foot,
And suddenly the horizon is hidden with ashes.

Since a Norman duke broke your gods of clay,
Always, under the laurel boughs of Virgil
The pale hydrangea joins the green myrtle!

HORUS

Le dieu Kneph en tremblant ébranlait l'univers:
Isis, la mère, alors se leva sur sa couche,
Fit un geste de haine à son époux farouche,
Et l'ardeur d'autrefois brilla dans ses yeux verts.

«Le voyez-vous, dit-elle, il meurt, ce vieux pervers,
Tous les frimas du monde ont passé par sa bouche,
Attachez son pied tors, éteignez son œil louche,
C'est le dieu des volcans et le roi des hivers!

L'aigle a déjà passé, l'esprit nouveau m'appelle,
J'ai revêtu pour lui la robe de Cybèle...
C'est l'enfant bien-aimé d'Hermès et d'Osiris!»

La Déesse avait fui sur sa conque dorée,
La mer nous renvoyait son image adorée,
Et les cieux rayonnaient sous l'écharpe d'Iris.

HORUS

The god Kneph in his trembling shook the universe:
Isis, the mother, then rose on her child-bed,
Made a gesture of hatred toward her savage mate,
And the ardor of the old days shone in her green eyes.

"Look at him," she said: "he dies, the old pervert!
All the frosts of the world have passt thru his mouth.
Bind his crookt foot, put out his crosst eye,
He is the god of volcanoes and the king of winters!

"The eagle has already passt, the new spirit calls me,
I have reclothed myself for him in the robe of Kybele...
He is the child beloved of Hermes and Osiris!"

The goddess had fled away upon her shell of gold,
The sea gave us back her adored image,
And the skies were radiant under the scarf of Iris.

ANTÉROS

Tu demandes pourquoi j'ai tant de rage au cœur
Et sur un col flexible une tête indomptée;
C'est que je suis issu de la race d'Antée,
Je retourne les dards contre le dieu vainqueur.

Oui, je suis de ceux-là qu'inspire le Vengeur,
Il m'a marqué le front de sa lèvre irritée,
Sous la pâleur d'Abel, hélas! ensanglantée,
J'ai parfois de Caïn l'implacable rougeur!

Jéhovah! le dernier, vaincu par ton génie,
Qui, du fond des enfers, criat: «Ô tyrannie!»
C'est mon aïeul Bélus ou mon père Dagon…

Ils m'ont plongé trois fois dans les eaux du Cocyte,
Et protégeant tout seul ma mère Amalécyte,
Je ressème à ses pieds les dents du vieux dragon.

ANTEROS

You ask why I have so much rage at heart
And upon a neck that could bend an unbowd head;
It's because I came from the race of Antaeus,
That I return the darts against the victorious god.

Yes, I am one of those whom the Avenger inspires,
He has markt my forehead with his inflamed lip,
Under the pallor of Abel, alas! staind with blood,
I have at times the irreconcilable blush of Cain.

Jehovah!   the last one, vanquisht by your genie,
Who from the pit of hell cried out: "O tyranny!"
That was my grandfather Belus or my father Dagon…

Three times they dipt me in the waters of Cocytus,
And, all alone protecting my mother the Amalekite,
I resow at her feet the teeth of the old dragon.

DELFICA

La connais-tu, DAFNÉ, cette ancienne romance,
Au pied du sycomore, ou sous les lauriers blancs,
Sous l'olivier, le myrthe ou les saules tremblants,
Cette chanson d'amour... qui toujours recommence!

Reconnais-tu le TEMPLE, au péristyle immense,
Et les citrons amers où s'imprimaient tes dents?
Et la grotte, fatale aux hôtes imprudents,
Où du dragon vaincu dort l'antique semence.

Ils reviendront ces dieux que tu pleures toujours!
Le temps va ramener l'ordre des anciens jours;
La terre a tressailli d'un souffle prophétique...

Cependant la sibylle au visage latin
Est endormie encor sous l'arc de Constatin:
— Et rien n'a dérangé le sévère portique.

DELPHICA

Do you know, DAPHNE, that song of the old days,
At the foot of the sycamore or under the white laurels,
Under the olive trees, the myrtle, or the trembling willows,
That song of love that always begins again?...

Do you still know the TEMPLE with its immense peristyle,
And the bitter lemons where your teeth presst their mark,
And the grotto, fatal to imprudent visitors,
Where the ancient seed of the vanquisht dragon sleeps?...

They will return, those Gods that you always weep for!
Time is going to bring back the order of the old days;
The earth has shudderd with a prophetic breath...

Meanwhile, the sibyl with the latin visage
Is still asleep beneath the Arch of Constantine
 — And nothing has disturbd the severe portico.

ARTÉMIS

La Treizième revient... C'est encor la première;
Et c'est toujours la seule, — ou c'est le seul moment:
Car est-tu reine, ô toi! la première ou dernière?
Es-tu roi, toi le seul ou le dernier amant?...

Aimez qui vous aima du berceau dans la bière;
Celle que j'aimai seul m'aime encor tendrement:
C'est la mort — ou la morte... Ô délice! ô tourment!
La rose qu'elle tient, c'est la *Rose trémière.*

Sainte napolitaine aux mains pleines de feux,
Rose au cœur violet, fleur de sainte Gudule:
As-tu trouvé ta croix dans le désert des cieux?

Roses blanches, tombez! vous insultez nos dieux:
Tombez fantômes blancs de votre ciel qui brûle:
— La sainte de l'abîme est plus sainte à mes yeux!

ARTEMIS

The Thirteenth returns... It is again She, the first one;
And She is always the One Alone, — or this is the only moment;
For art thou queen, O thou! the first or last?
Art thou king, thou the only or the last lover?...

Love who loved you from the cradle to the grave;
She that I loved alone loves me still tenderly:
She is Death — or the Dead One... O delite! O torment!
The rose that she holds is the *Rose hollyhock.*

Neapolitan saint with hands full of fires,
Rose violet at the heart, flower of Saint Gudule:
Didst thou find thy cross in the desert of the skies?

White roses, fall! you insult our gods.
Fall, white phantoms, from your sky that burns:
— The saint of the abyss is more saintly to my eyes!

Dieu est mort! le ciel est vide...
Pleurez! enfants, vous n'avez plus de père!
— Jean-Paul

LE CHRIST AUX OLIVIERS

I

Quand le Seigneur, levant au ciel ses maigres bras,
Sous les arbres sacrés, comme font les poètes,
Se fut longtemps perdu dans ses douleurs muettes,
Et se jugea trahi par des amis ingrats;

Il se tourna vers ceux qui l'attendaient en bas
Rêvant d'être des rois, des sage, des prophètes...
Mais engourdis, perdus dans le sommeil des bêtes,
Et se prit à crier: «Non, Dieu n'existe pas!»

Ils dormaient. «Mes amis, savez-vous *la nouvelle?*
J'ai touché de mon front à la voûte éternelle;
Je suis sanglant, brisé, souffrant pour bien des jours!

Frère, je vous trompais: Abîme! abîme! abîme!
Le dieu manque à l'autel, où je suis la victime...
Dieu n'est pas! Dieu n'est plus!» Mais ils dormaient toujours!

God is dead! the sky is empty...
Weep! children, you no longer have a father!
— Jean Paul Richter

THE CHRIST IN THE OLIVE GROVE

I

When the Lord, lifting to the sky his thin arms,
Under the sacred trees, as poets do,
Had been for a long time lost in his mute sorrows,
And believed himself betrayd by ungrateful friends;

He turnd towards those who waited for him below
Dreaming of being kings, sages, prophets...
But dull with it, lost in the beasts' sleep,
And he began to cry out: "No, God does not exist!"

They slept.   "Friends, do you know the *tidings?*
I have toucht my forehead to the eternal vault;
I am broken, bloody, too long suffering!

"Brothers, I deceived you: Abyss!   abyss!   abyss!
The god is missing from the altar where I am the victim...
There is no God!   God no longer exists!"   But they still slept...

II

Il reprit: «Tout est mort! J'ai parcouru les mondes;
Et j'ai perdu mon vol dans leurs chemins lactés,
Aussi loin que la vie, en ses veines fécondes,
Répand des sables d'or et des flots argentés:

Partout le sol désert côtoyé par des ondes,
Des tourbillons confus d'océans agités...
Un souffle vague émeut les sphères vagabondes,
Mais nul esprit n'existe en ces immensités.

En cherchant l'œil de Dieu, je n'ai vu qu'un orbite
Vaste, noir et sans fond; d'où la nuit qui l'habite
Rayonne sur le monde et s'épaissit toujours;

Un arc-en-ciel étrange entoure ce puits sombre,
Seuil de l'ancien chaos dont le néant est l'ombre,
Spirale, engloutissant les Mondes et les Jours!»

II

He began again: "Everything is dead! I have searcht the worlds;
And I have lost my flight in their milky ways,
As far as life, in its prolific veins,
Pours out the golden sands and floods of silver.

"Everywhere, the desert soil borderd by waves,
Confused whirlpools of disturbd oceans...
A vague breath moves the wandering spheres
But no spirit exists in those immensities.

"Looking for the eye of God, I saw only a socket,
Vast, black, and bottomless, from whence the Night that dwells there
Streams out over the world and ever deepens;

"A strange rainbow encircles this somber pit,
Threshold of the old chaos whose shadow is nothingness,
Spiral engulfing the Worlds and Days!"

III

«Immobile Destin, muette sentinelle,
Froide Nécessité!... Hasard qui t'avançant,
Parmi les mondes morts sous la neige éternelle,
Refroidis, par degrés l'univers pâlissant,

Sais-tu ce que tu fais, puissance originelle,
De tes soleils éteints, l'un l'autre se froissant...
Es-tu sûr de transmettre une haleine immortelle,
Entre un monde qui meurt et l'autre renaissant?...

Ô mon père! est-ce toi que je sens en moi-même?
As-tu pouvoir de vivre et de vaincre la mort?
Aurais-tu succombé sous un dernier effort

De cet ange des nuits que frappa l'anathème...
Car je me sens tout seul à pleurer et souffrir,
Hélas! et si je meurs, c'est que tout va mourir!»

III

"Immovable Fate, mute sentinel,
Cold Necessity!...Chance, who, advancing
Among the dead worlds under the eternal snow,
Chills by degrees the paling universe,

"Do you know what you are doing, primordial power,
With your extinguisht suns, falling upon one another...
Are you sure of transmitting an immortal breath
Between a world that dies and another being born again?...

"O my father! is it thee that I sense in myself?
Hast thou the power to live and to conquer death?
Wilt thou have succumbd under the last effort

"Of that angel of nights whom the anathema struck?...
For I sense myself alone in my weeping and suffering,
Alas! and, if I die, everything is going to die!"

IV

Nul n'entendait gémir l'éternelle victime,
Livrant au monde en vain tout son cœur épanché;
Mais prêt à défaillir et sans force penché,
Il appela le *seul* — éveillé dans Solyme:

«Judas! lui cria-t-il, tu sais ce qu'on m'estime,
Hâte-toi de me vendre, et finis ce marché:
Je suis souffrant, ami! sur la terre couché…
Viens! ô toi qui, du moins, as la force du crime!»

Mais Judas s'en allait mécontent et pensif,
Se trouvant mal payé, plein d'un remords si vif
Qu'il lisait ses noirceurs sur tous les murs écrites…

Enfin Pilate seul, qui veillait pour César,
Sentant quelque pitié, se tourna par hasard:
«Allez chercher ce fou!» dit-il aux satellites.

I V

No one heard the eternal victim groan,
Giving up to the world in vain all his pour'd-out heart;
But, ready to faint and reeling without strength,
He call'd upon the *one alone* — awake in Jerusalem:

"Judas!" he cried to him: "You know how they value me,
Make haste and sell me, and finish this haggling:
I am suffering, Friend!   beaten to the ground.
Come!   O you who, at least, have the strength of crime!"

But Judas went his way, discontent and brooding,
Finding himself badly paid, full of a remorse so alive
That he read his black deeds written on every wall...

At last, Pilate alone, who kept vigil for Caesar,
Feeling some pity, turn'd by chance:
"Go look for this madman!" he commanded his satellites.

V

C'était bien lui, ce fou, cet insensé sublime...
Cet Icare oublié qui remontait les cieux,
Ce Phaéton perdu sous la foudre des dieux,
Ce bel Atys meurtri que Cybèle ranime!

L'augure interrogeait le flanc de la victime,
La terre s'enivrait de ce sang précieux...
L'univers étourdi penchait sur ses essieux,
Et l'Olympe un instant chancela vers l'abîme.

«Réponds! criait César à Jupiter Ammon,
Quel est ce nouveau dieu qu'on impose à la terre?
Et si ce n'est un dieu, c'est au moins un démon... »

Mais l'oracle invoqué pour jamais dut se taire;
Un seul pouvait au monde expliquer ce mystère:
— Celui qui donna l'âme aux enfants du limon.

V

It was him all right, this madman, this sublime insensate...
This forgotten Icarus climbing the skies again,
This Phaethon destroyd under the divine thunderbolt,
This beautiful murderd Atys whom Kybele reanimates!

The augur examined the side-wound of the victim,
The earth became drunk with that precious blood...
The stunnd universe reeld upon its axles,
And Olympus for an instant staggerd toward the Abyss.

"Answer!" cried Caesar to Jupiter Ammon:
"Who is this new god that is imposed on the earth?
And if this be not a god, it is at least a daemon..."

But the oracle invoked had to be forever silent;
One alone could explain this mystery to the world:
— He who gave soul to the children of the clay.

Eh quoi! tout est sensible!
— Pythagore

VERS DORÉS

Homme, libre penseur! te crois-tu seul pensant
Dans ce monde où la vie éclate en toute chose?
Des forces que tu tiens ta liberté dispose,
Mais de tous tes conseils l'univers est absent.

Respecte dans la bête un esprit agissant:
Chaque fleur est une âme à la Nature éclose;
Un mystère d'amour dans le métal repose;
«Tout est sensible!» Et tout sur ton être est puissant.

Crains, dans le mur aveugle, un regard qui t'épie:
À la matière même un verbe est attaché…
Ne la fais pas servir à quelque usage impie!

Souvent dans l'être obscur habite un Dieu caché;
Et comme un œil naissant couvert par ses paupières,
Un pur esprit s'accroît sous l'écorce des pierres!

GOLDEN LINES

Man, free thinker! do you believe yourself the one alone thinking
In this world where life bursts forth in everything?
Your free will disposes of the forces that you hold
But in all your councils the universe is absent.

Respect in the animal an active intellect:
Each flower is a soul in Nature bloomd forth;
A mystery of love lies conceald in the metal;
"Everything is sentient!"
            Everything has power over your being.

Beware in the blind wall a gaze that watches you:
To matter itself a voice is in-bound...
Do not make it serve some impious use!

Often in the obscure being dwells a hidden God;
And like a nascent eye coverd by its lids
A pure spirit grows beneath the skin of stones.

PANDORA

Alas! Two spirits divide my soul, and each wants to separate from the other: one, burning with love, is bound to the world by the body; a numinous longing beckons the other spirit away from this darkness, carrying it up to where our ancestors dwell.

— FAUST [1]

O my friends, you have all known her! The lovely Pandora of the Viennese Theater. She has left you, no doubt, as she left me, with cruel and sweet memories! It is perhaps to her — it is certainly to her — that one could apply the incomprehensible enigma engraved upon the stone of Bologna: ÆLIA LÆLIA. *Nec vir, nec mulier, nec androgyna,* etc. "Neither man, nor woman, nor androgyne, nor daughter, nor young, nor old, nor *chaste,* nor *mad,* nor modest, but all this together…" In a word, *Pandora,* that says it all, for I don't wish to say everything.[2]

O well-guarded Vienna! The paladins' rock of love, as old Menzel named you — you do not possess the mystical Holy Grail, but rather, the *Stock-im-Eisen* of the brave guildsmen. Swords are irresistibly drawn toward your magnetic mountain, and the jealous Magyar, the intrepid Bohemian, and the noble Lombard would all give their lives in your defense at the divine feet of *Maria Hilf!*

I, myself, was unable to hammer the symbolic nail into the iron-laden trunk (*Stock-im-Eisen*) which stands at the entryway to the *Graben,* in front of the jeweler's shop; but I poured my sweetest tears and the purest effusions of my heart along the squares and the streets, upon the bastions, along the paths of the Augarten and in the groves of the Prater. The timorous doe and the domestic pheasant were moved to pity by my love songs. I strolled, day-dreaming, over the grassy slopes of the Schönbrunn. I adored the pale statues in those gardens crowning Maria Theresa's *Gloriette.* My heart was ravished by the Chimeras of the old palace as I admired their divine eyes, longing to suck at their radiant breasts of marble.[3]

Forgive my having caught a glance from your beautiful eyes, august Archduchess. I was so in love with your image, painted as it was upon the shop sign. You reminded me of the other... that dream of my youth, which so often led me from my home to the town of the Stuarts! I would go on foot, traversing plains and woods, dreaming of Diane of the Valois, protégé of the Medicis. Above the houses of Pecq and the pavilion of Henri IV, I could make out the brick towers with their stringcourses of slate; then I would cross the Seine which languished and curled round its islands, and enter the solemn ruins of the old Château de Saint-Germain. The gloomy appearance of the high porticos, the soaring bats, the lizards running off, and the young goats leaping about, nibbling on the green acanthus, filled me with joy and love. Then, when I reached the mountain's plateau, what happiness it was, despite the wind and the storm, to see beyond the houses the bluish hillside of Mareil, and its church where the ashes of the old Lord Monteynard rest!

The recollection of my lovely cousins, those intrepid huntresses of bygone days with whom I strolled in the woods, both as beautiful as the daughters of Leda, overwhelms and intoxicates me still.

All the same, I loved only her, *in those days!*...[4]

It was very cold in Vienna, the last day of the year, and I was enjoying myself in Pandora's boudoir. She was scarcely making any progress in the letter she was pretending to write, and her charming spidery writing weaved madly with the mysterious arpeggios that she occasionally pulled from the strings of her harp, whose head vanished under the interlacings of a gilded siren.

All of a sudden, she threw herself at my neck and kissed me, saying with a mad laugh:

"Look, it's a little priest! He is much more amusing than my baron."

I went to the mirror to fix myself up, for my auburn hair had become uncurled, and I blushed with humiliation, realizing I was loved only because of a certain ecclesiastical air lent by my timid manner and black coat.

"Pandora," I said to her, "let's not joke about love or religion, for they really are the same thing."

"But I adore priests," she said. "Let me have my illusion."

"Pandora," I said bitterly, "I will no longer wear this black coat, and when I next come to see you, I will wear my blue coat with gold buttons, the one that gives me such a cavalier appearance."

"I will only receive you in a black coat," she said. And she called for her attendant:

"Röschen!... If that gentleman there presents himself in a blue coat, you will show him out and bar him from the hotel. — I have had quite enough," she added angrily, "of embassy attachés dressed in blue with their coronet buttons, and officers of his Imperial Majesty, and Magyars with their velvet clothes and their feathered hats. That little one there will suit me quite well as a priest. Goodbye my priest, it's settled, you will come for me tomorrow by coach and we will go to the Prater... and you will be wearing black!"

Each word entered my heart like a thorn. An engagement, an actual engagement for the following day, the first day of the year; and what was more, I was to be dressed in black. And it was not so much the black coat that made me despair, but my empty purse. What a disgrace! Empty, alas! The very day of the new year!...

Driven by a mad hope, I hurried to the post office to see whether my uncle had sent me a registered letter.

O joy! They asked me for two florins and handed over an epistle that bore a French stamp. A ray of sunlight beat straight down upon this insidious letter. The merciless lines it revealed did not carry the slightest mention of a money order or bill of exchange. It obviously held nothing but moral maxims and pieces of economic advice.

I handed it back, pretending to have taken the wrong vest, and with a feigned surprise I struck my pockets which failed to emit any metallic sound; I then plunged into the crowded streets that surround Saint Stephen's.

Fortunately, I had a friend in Vienna: a very nice fellow, a little mad like all Germans, a doctor of philosophy who charmingly cultivated a slight aptitude for the role of light tenor.

I knew I could find him at the home of his mistress, Rosa, an extra at the Leopoldstadt theater. He paid her a visit every day from 2 to 5 o'clock. I quickly passed through the Rothenthor and walked to the suburb. At the bottom of the stairs I could hear the voice of my comrade singing in a languorous tone:

> *Einen Kuss von rosiger Lippe,*
> *Und ich fürchte nicht Sturm und nicht Klippe!*[5]

The poor devil was accompanying himself on the guitar with the air of a minstrel, something not yet considered ridiculous in Vienna. I took him aside and explained my situation.

"You realize," he said, "that it's New Year's Eve..."

"Oh! Fair enough!" I exclaimed, catching sight of a lavish display of flower-filled vases upon Rosa's mantelpiece. "Then there's nothing left to do but put a knife in my heart, or head toward Lobau Island, where the strongest branches of the Danube can be found..."

"Wait a moment," he said, taking my arm.

We left. He said to me:

"I salvaged this from Dalilah's hands... Here you are, two Austrian crowns; use them carefully. Try not to spend them before tomorrow!"

I crossed the snow-covered banks and returned to Leopoldstadt where I was staying among the laundresses. There I found a letter reminding me that I was to participate in a brilliant performance, to be attended by some diplomats and members of the court. It mentioned a possibility of a game of charades. I resigned myself to the part irritably, for I had barely studied it. Kathi came to see me, cheery and dressed up, *bionda grassota,* as always, and told me charming things in her dialect, a mixture of Moravian and Venetian. I was not quite sure what flower she was wearing upon her bodice. I asked if I might have it, hoping she would give it to me out of kindness. She told me in a tone of voice that was new to me:

"Not for less than *zehn Gulden-Conventions-münze!"* (ten florins in standard currency).

I acted as if I didn't understand. She left in a huff, telling me she would go find her old baron who would give her costlier New Year's gifts.

I was free. I walked through the suburb learning my role, which I held in my hand. I ran into Wahby the Bohemian, who gave me a languishing look full of reproach. I felt a need to have dinner at the Rothenthor, where I flooded my stomach with a red Tokay at three kreutzers a glass, washing down some grilled cutlets, *Wurschell* and a dish of snails.

The glowing shops were overflowing with ladies shopping and thousands of frills and furbelows; revelers and Nuremberg dolls exchanged fixed grins through the window displays, to the accompaniment of an infantile chorus of Basque drums and tin trumpets.

"Wretched candy consultant!" I exclaimed, remembering Hoffmann.

And I quickly descended the worn steps of the *Hunter's* Tavern. They were singing the poet Zedlitz's *Nocturnal Revue.* The great shadow of the emperor hovered over the joyous gathering, and I hummed to myself:

O Richard!...

A charming girl brought me a glass of *Bayerisch Bier,* but I did not dare kiss her, for I was thinking of my next day's engagement.

I could not keep still. I escaped from the tumultuous joy of the tavern, and went to have my coffee at the Graben. As I crossed Saint Stephen's Square, a good-hearted old bootblack recognized me and cried out, as she always did: "S*** n*** de D***!" — the only words of French she remembered from the imperial invasion.

These words reminded me of my evening's performance; I had been about to settle into a stall at the Kärntnerther Theater to admire Mlle Lutzer, as was my custom. I had my shoes shined, for the snow had really spoiled them.

A good cup of coffee picked me up enough to present myself at the Palace. The streets were filled with costumed Lombards, Bohemians and Hungarians. Diamonds, rubies and opals sparkled on their breasts, and most of them were making their way toward the *Burg* to pay their respects to the imperial family.

I did not dare join this boisterous crowd; but the cherished memory of the other... still protected me from the deceitful Pandora's charms.

When I arrived at the French Embassy they told me I was very late. The irritated Pandora was amusing herself by toying with an old baron and a young prince who was grotesquely dressed as a student at the carnival. This young *fox*[6] had stolen from the office a cheap candle which he had fashioned into a dagger. He was menacing the tyrants with it while declaiming verses of tragedy and invoking the shade of Schiller.

To kill time, we decided to play an *impromptu* game of charades. — The first word was *Maréchal.*[7] The first clue was *marée.*[8] — Vatel, in the guise of a young embassy attaché, uttered a soliloquy before plunging the point of his ceremonial sword into his heart.[9] After that, an amiable diplomat paid a visit to his ladylove; he held a quatrain in his hand and was letting the fringe of a *shawl* hang out from the pocket of his coat. "Enough, that's all I need!" (that *shawl* I need) said the cunning Pandora as she pulled to her the genuine Biétry cashmere, allegedly *woven* in Golconda.[10] She then performed the dance of the shawl with an adorable carelessness. Then the third scene began and we saw a renowned *marshal* appear wearing an historical hat.[11]

We continued with another charade whose word was *mandarin*. — This one began with a *mandat*[12] that I was asked to sign, upon which I wrote the glorious name of Macaire (Robert), Baron des Adrets, the overly delicate Éloa's second husband. I was heartily applauded for this bit of buffoonery. The second term of the charade was *Rhin*.[13] Someone sang the verses of Alfred de Musset. All this naturally lead to the arrival of a genuine *mandarin* draped in cashmere, who, legs crossed, was lazily smoking a hookah. — The seductive Pandora still needed to play a trick of her own. She appeared in the lightest of costumes, wearing a loose white blouse embroidered with garnets and a flowing dress of Scottish fabric. Her dark hair was plaited in the form of a lyre and stood like two majestic horns upon her head. Like an angel she sang Déjazet's romance: *I am Tching-Ka!...*

The three knocks were finally sounded for the proverb entitled *Madame Sorbet*. I appeared as a provincial comedian, like *Destiny* in the *Roman comique*.[14] My cold *Star* soon realized that I did not know a word of my part and took pleasure in confusing me even further. The icy smile of the ladies in the audience greeted my opening scene and filled me with terror. The viscount exhausted himself in vain prompting me with M. Théodore Leclerq's exquisite lines. I ruined the performance.[15]

In anger, I knocked over the folding screen which depicted a country salon. — What a scandal! I fled the room as fast as I could, rushing down the staircases, pushing my way through crowds of ushers with silver chains and servants in striped Hungarian uniforms, and, with the *legs of a deer,*[16] I bounded in disgrace for the *Hunter's* Tavern to take refuge.

There, I asked for a jug of new wine, which I blended with a jug of aged wine, and I wrote a four-page letter to the goddess in an abracadabraesque style. — I reminded her of Prometheus's sufferings when he brought to light a creature as depraved as her. I criticized her box of tricks and her bayadere clothing. I even dared attack her serpentine feet, which I had seen slip insidiously under her dress. — Then I took the letter to her hotel.

I returned to my small lodging at Leopoldstadt, but I was unable to sleep that night. I kept seeing her dancing with her two carved silver horns, swinging her plumed head, her goffered lace collar rippling upon her brocaded dress.

How beautiful she was in her silk clothing and scarlet levantine, her white shoulders insolently glistening, oiled with the sweat of the world. For a moment I almost yielded to her dangerous caresses, when it seemed to me I had seen her before at the dawn of the centuries.[17]

"Miserable woman!" I said. "We are lost because of you, and the world is going to end! Aren't you aware that one can no longer breathe here? The air is contaminated with your poisons and the last candle which still shines upon us is already flickering and growing dim from our impure breath... Air! Some air! We're dying!"

"My lord," she cried, "we have only seven thousand years to live. That only makes one thousand one hundred and forty..."

"Seventy-seven thousand," I said to her, "and still millions of years more: your necromancers are wrong!"

Then she soared, rejuvenated, from the flashy garments that covered her, and her flight disappeared into the crimson sky of the fourposter bed. My drifting spirit tried in vain to follow her: she had vanished for all eternity.

I was in the midst of swallowing some pomegranate seeds. This absent-mindedness gave way to a painful sensation in my throat. I found myself choking. My head was severed and put on display at the doorway of a seraglio, and I truly would have died if a parrot, passing by in full flight, had not swallowed some of the seeds which were mingled with blood.

It carried me to Rome under the blossoming arbor of the Vatican's trellis, where the lovely Imperia sat enthroned at the sacred table, surrounded by a conclave of cardinals. At the sight of the golden plates, I felt alive again, and said to her: "I know very well who you are, Jezebel!" There was then a cracking in the hall. It was the announcement of the *Deluge,* an opera in three acts. It then seemed to me that my spirit was piercing the earth, and, swimming through the coral banks of Oceania and the crimson sea of the tropics, I found myself cast upon the shaded beach of the Isle of Love. It was the shore of Tahiti. Three young women surrounded me and little by little brought me back to life. I addressed them. They had forgotten the language of man: "Greetings my heavenly sisters," I said to them, smiling.

I threw myself out of bed like a madman — it was broad daylight; I had to wait until noon to discover my letter's effect. Pandora was still asleep when I arrived at her hotel. She leapt with joy and said: "Let's go to the Prater, I'll get dressed." While I was waiting for her in her drawing room, Prince *** knocked on the door. He told me he was returning from the castle. I had thought him to be at his estates. — He talked for a while of his skill with the sword, and of certain rapiers that the students of the north use in their duels. We were fencing in the air, when our double Star appeared. The trick then was to not be the one who left the room. They started to converse in a language unknown to me; but I held my ground. The three of us went down the stairs together, and the prince accompanied us all the way to the entrance of the Kohlmarkt.

"You've done beautifully," she said to me. "Germany shall be on fire for a century."

I accompanied her to her music shop; as she was leafing through the albums, I saw the old marquis running up in a Magyar's uniform, but without the hat, exclaiming: "What imprudence! The two fools are going to kill each other for your sake!" I put an end to this ridiculous conversation by hailing a carriage. Pandora gave orders for the Dorotheergasse, to her milliner's. She stayed in there for an hour, then said as she left: "I am surrounded by idiots."

"And me?" I asked humbly.

"Oh, you! You're at the top of the list."

"Thank you!" I replied.

I spoke confusedly of the Prater; but the wind had changed. In disgrace I had to bring her back to her hotel, and my two Austrian crowns were barely sufficient to pay for the carriage.

In a rage, I went and shut myself in my room, where I had a fever. The next morning, I received a short letter enjoining me to learn the part of Valbelle, for a performance of the play entitled *Some Words in the Forest.* — I was wary of subjecting myself to another humiliation, and set off for Salzburg, where I went to reflect bitterly in the old house of Mozart, now occupied by a chocolate maker.

I did not see Pandora again until the following year, in a cold capital up north. Her carriage suddenly stopped in the middle of the great square, and a divine smile nailed me helplessly to the ground. "You again, enchantress," I exclaimed, "and the fatal box, what have you done with it?"

"I've filled it for you," she said, "with the most beautiful toys of

Nuremberg. Won't you come admire them?"

But I began to flee as fast as I could towards the financial district. "O son of the gods, father of man!" she was crying out. "Wait a moment. It's New Year's Eve, just like last year... Where have you hidden the fire of heaven that you stole from Jupiter?"

I did not want to answer. I have always particularly disliked the name of Prometheus, for I still feel at my side the eternal beak of the vulture from whom Alcide delivered me.

O Jupiter! When will my torture end?

WALKS AND MEMORIES

I

THE SLOPES OF MONTMARTRE

It is extremely difficult to find housing in Paris. — I have never been so convinced of this as in these last two months. Having arrived from Germany, I set about, after a brief sojourn at a villa in the suburbs, to find myself a home more secure than my previous ones, the first of which had been located at the Place du Louvre and the other at the Rue du Mail. — This is only going back six years. — Evicted from the former with twenty francs compensation, which I neglected, I do not know why, to go claim from the city, I found in the latter that which one hardly finds anymore in the heart of Paris: — a view of two or three trees occupying a fair amount of space, allowing one to breathe and to relax the mind by looking at something other than a chessboard of dark windows, in which attractive faces only appear by exception. —

I respect the private life of my neighbors, and am not one of those who examine by telescope the curves of a woman going to bed, or observe with the naked eye the silhouettes particular to the incidents and minor events of married life. — I much prefer a view "utterly pleasing to the eyes," as Fénelon would say, which one can enjoy at either sunrise or sunset, but particularly sunrise. I am less concerned with sunset, as I am always sure to find it away from home. But as for sunrise, that is different: I love seeing the sun carve out angles on the walls, hearing the chirpings of birds outside, be they simple sparrows… Grétry offered a louis to hear a *chanterelle.*[1] I would give twenty francs for a blackbird; — the twenty francs which the city of Paris still owes me!

I lived for a long time in Montmartre; the air is very pure there, the landscapes are varied, providing one with magnificent views, whether "through having been virtuous, one enjoys seeing the dawn rise," which is very beautiful around Paris, or whether with less simple tastes one prefers those crimson hues of the west, where the ragged and drifting clouds paint scenes of battle and transfiguration above the great cemetery, between the Arc de l'Étoile and the bluish hills which go from Argenteuil to Pontoise. — The new houses are always advancing, like the diluvian sea which bathed the sides of the ancient mountain, seeping bit by bit into the lairs in which the misshapen monsters, reconstructed since by Cuvier, had taken refuge. — Attacked on one side by the Rue de l'Empereur, on the other by the city hall district, which undermines the uneven slopes and lowers the heights of Paris's hills, the old Mont de Mars will soon share the fate of the Butte des Moulins, which last century displayed a scarcely less magnificent front. — Yet a fair number of hills still remain, encircled with thick green hedges, decorated in turn by the violet flowers and crimson berries of the Barbery. There are also mills, taverns and arbors, elysian fields and quiet alleys lined with thatched cottages, barns and lush gardens, green plains cut with chasms, in which the springs seep through the clay, detaching little by little some islets of greenery on which goats gambol about, grazing on the acanthus hanging from the rocks. Little girls with proud eyes and sturdy feet watch over them while playing amongst themselves. There is even a vineyard, the last of the famous vintage of

Montmartre, who in the time of the Romans fought with Argenteuil and Suresnes. Each year this humble hillside loses a row of its shriveled stock, which falls into a quarry. — Ten years ago, I could have purchased it for three thousand francs... Today they are asking thirty thousand. It has the loveliest view in the vicinity of Paris.

What charmed me most in this small area shaded by the large trees of the Château des Brouillards, was the remaining vineyard linked to the memory of Saint Denis, who, from the standpoint of the philosophers, was perhaps the second Bacchus (Διονύσιος),[2] and who had three bodies, the first of which is buried at Montmartre, the second at Ratisbonne and the third at Corinthe. — Following that, it was the proximity of the watering place, which comes to life in the evening with all the horses and dogs that are brought there to bathe, and a fountain built in the ancient style, where the washerwomen chat and sing as in one of the first chapters of *Werther*. With a bas-relief consecrated to Diana, and perhaps two figures of naiads sculpted in demirelief, one would obtain, in the shade of the old lime trees which lean over the monument, a wonderful place of retreat, quiet at certain moments, and which would recall certain sketches of the Roman countryside. Above, one can see the Rue des Brouillards, snaking down to the Chemin des Boeufs, then the garden of the Gaucher restaurant, with its pavilions, its lanterns and painted statues. — The outlines of the Saint-Denis plain are wonderful, bordered by the hills of Saint-Ouen and Montmorency, with flashes of sunlight or clouds which change every hour of the day. To the right is a row of houses, the majority of them shut up on account of the cracks in the walls. It is this that ensures the relative stillness of this setting: for the horses and oxen which pass by, and even the washerwomen, do not disturb the meditations of a wise man, and even coalesce. — Bourgeois life, its interests and mundane affairs, only inspire him to withdraw as far as possible from the great centers of activity.

To the left, vast terrains cover the site of a caved-in quarry, which the town gave away to some industrious men who have transformed it. They planted trees, created fields green with potatoes and beets, on which the rising asparagus recently stretched out its green plumes decorated with red pearls.

Going down the path, one turns left. Another two or three green hills come into view, cut through by a road which further on descends into the deep ravines, and which endeavors to one day join the Rue de l'Empereur between the hills and the cemetery. There one can find a hamlet that smacks strongly of the countryside, and which until three years ago carried out the unwholesome work of a *night soil* workshop. — Today the people there use the residue of stearic candles. — How many artists, turned down for the Prix de Rome, have come to this spot to study the Roman countryside and the aspect of the Pontine marshes! There even remains a marsh lively with ducks, goslings and hens.

It is also not uncommon to come across picturesque old clothes on the backs of workers. The hills, cleaved through here and there, accentuate the land's settlement upon the old quarries; but nothing is lovelier than the look of the great hill, when the sun shines down upon its terrain of red ochre veined with lime and clay, its bare rocks and some bunches of trees still covered with a thick foliage, through which ravines and paths meander. Most of the terrain and the scattered houses of this little valley belong to old landowners, who are counting on the predicament of Parisians needing to create new homes for themselves, and the tendency of the houses of the Montmartre district to invade, over time, the Saint-Denis plain. A lock checks the torrent; when it opens, the land will be very valuable. — I regret all the more having hesitated, ten years ago, in handing over three thousand francs for the last vineyard of Montmartre.

There is no more use thinking about it. I will never be a landowner; and yet how many times, on the 8th or the 15th of each quarter (around Paris, at any rate), have I sung the refrain of M. Vautour:

When one does not have enough to pay one's rent
One must have a house of one's own!

I would have constructed such a light building in this vineyard!... A little villa in the style of Pompeii, with an *impluvium* and a *cella*, something like the house of the tragic poet. Poor Laviron, who died at the walls of Rome, had drawn out the plan for me. — Yet to tell the truth, there are no landowners on the hills of Montmartre. One cannot legally establish ownership on this terrain undermined by the cavities populated with mammoths and mastodons on their inner walls. The town concedes a right of possession which expires after a hundred years... They are camped out like Turks; and the most progressive tenets would hardly contest such a transient claim, in which the right of inheritance cannot become established at length.[*]

---

[*]Certain landowners repudiate this detail, something which I have heard others affirm. Would this not also result in usurpations similar to those which gave back hereditary fiefs under Hugues Capet!

II

THE CHÂTEAU DE SAINT-GERMAIN

I visited all the quarters of Paris in which I had friends, but found nothing but impossible prices, augmented by the conditions set out by the concierges. After finally finding housing for under three hundred francs, I was asked if I had a condition which demanded daylight. — I believe I replied that my health demanded it. — "I ask," the concierge told me, "because the window of the room opens onto a passage which is not very well lit." I did not need to know any more, and I even neglected to look over a *basement for rent,* remembering that I had seen this same inscription in London, followed by the words: "For a single gentleman."

I asked myself: "Why not go live at Versailles or Saint-Germain?" The suburbs are even more expensive than Paris; but, with a season ticket for the railroad, one could probably find housing in the most deserted or abandoned parts of these two towns. In fact, what is half an hour on the railroad in the morning and evening? One would have a city's resources, while practically living in the country. You would actually be living at Rue Saint-Lazare, no. 130.[3] The journey is quite pleasant, and as far as tedium or fatigue goes, is nothing like a trip by omnibus. — I was very pleased with this idea, and I chose Saint-Germain, which for me is a town filled with memories. What a delightful journey! Asnières, Chatou, Nanterre and Le Pecq; the thrice-coiled Seine, views of green islands, of plains, woods, of chalets and villas; on the right, the hills of Colombes, Argenteuil and Carrières; on the left, the Valérian mountain, Bougival, Luciennes and Marly; and then the loveliest view in the world: the terrace and the old galleries of the castle of Henry IV, crowned with the stern outline of the castle of Francis I. I have always loved this bizarre castle, which from above has the shape of a Gothic *D,* in honor, it is said, of the lovely Diana. — I only regret not seeing those great roofs scaled with slate, those openwork pinnacles in which staircases uncoil in spirals, those tall sculpted windows thrusting up from a jumble of angular roofs which are so characteristic of the architecture of the Valois. Under Louis XVIII, masons disfigured the side which faces the gardens. Since then, this building has been converted into a penitentiary, and the effect of the moats and ancient bridges has been spoiled by an enclosure of high walls covered in public notices. The tall windows and the gilded balconies, the terraces on which the fair beauties of the court of the Valois and the Stuarts, the gallant knights of the Médicis and the loyal Scots of Marie Stuart and King James all appeared in their turn, have never been restored; nothing remains but the noble design of the openings, the towers and the facades, but this strange contrast of brick and slate, lit by the fiery glow of the west or the silvery light of the night, and this appearance, half-romantic, half-warlike, of a fortified castle, containing within itself a splendid palace set upon a mountain, between a wooded valley through which a river snakes, and a flowerbed outlined at the edge of a vast forest.

I was returning, like Ravenswood to the castle of his fathers; I had had relatives among the occupants of this castle — this is already twenty years ago; some others among the town's inhabitants; four tombs in all... and mingling with these impressions are the remembrances of love and holidays going back to the time of the Bourbons; — so that I was alternately happy and sad the whole evening!

A mundane incident tore me from the poetry of these dreams of youth.

Night had fallen, and, having wandered through the streets and squares, saluted the dwellings I once loved and taken a last quick look at the sites of L'Étang, Mareil and Chambourcy, I was finally resting in a café which looks onto the market place. I was served a mug of beer. At the bottom were three woodlice; — a man who has lived in the Orient is incapable of being upset by such a detail: "Waiter!" I said, "it is quite possible that I like woodlice; but next time, if I ask for them, I would like them served on the side." The saying was not new, being usually applied to the hairs served on an omelette —but it might still be appreciated in Saint-Germain. The customers, butchers or drovers, found it agreeable.

The waiter, unperturbed, replied: "Sir, this shouldn't surprise you: they are presently restoring the castle, and these insects take refuge in the town. They are very fond of beer and make it their grave."

"Waiter," I said to him, "you are a most excellent fellow and your speech has won me over... But is this true that they're restoring the castle?"

"I believe the gentleman has just been so informed."

"Informed thanks to your reasoning; but are you certain of the fact itself?"

"It's what the papers say."

Having long been away from France, I could not question this testimony. The following day, I went to the castle to see at what stage the restoration was at. The sergeant-concierge said to me, with a smile one finds only on a soldier of this rank: "Sir, just to reinforce the castle's foundations would take nine million; do you have that kind of money?"

I have reached the point where nothing surprises me anymore: "I don't have it on me," I remarked, "but it could still be found!"

"Well!" he said. "When you find it, we'll show you the castle."

I was piqued; so much so that I returned to Saint-Germain two days later. An idea had occurred to me: Why not, I asked myself, start a fund? France is poor: but many English will be coming next year for the exposition on the Champs-Élysées. It is impossible that they would not aid us in saving from destruction a castle which lodged several generations of their kings and queens. All the Jacobite families passed through there — even today the town is still half English; as a child I sang the songs of King James and mourned Mary Stuart, declaiming the verse of Ronsard and Du Bellay... The race of King Charles fills the streets like a still-living proof of the attachments to so many vanished races... No! I told myself, the English cannot refuse to join us in a fund doubly national. If we contribute some cash, they will assuredly come up with some crowns and guineas!

Confident of this scheme, I went to submit it to the customers at the market café. They received it with enthusiasm, and when I asked for a mug of beer *without woodlice,* the waiter said to me: "Oh no, sir! Not today!"

I went to the castle with my head held high. The sergeant ushered me into the guardroom, where I elaborated upon my idea with success, and the commander, once informed, was happy to have them show me the chapel and the apartments of the Stuarts, closed off to those simply sightseeing. These apartments are in a sad state, and as for the galleries, the ancient halls and the bedrooms of the Medicis, it is impossible to recognize them from how they must have been centuries ago, thanks to the walls, the masonry and the fake ceilings which adapted this castle to the army's needs.

How beautiful the courtyard is, all the same! The sculpted contours, the arches, the chivalrous galleries, even the irregularity of the layout, the red tint of the facades, all this makes me muse on the castles of Scotland and Ireland, of Walter Scott and Byron. They have done so much for Versailles and Fontainbleau… then why not rebuild these precious ruins of our history? The curse of Catherine de Médicis, jealous of the monument built in honor of Diana, continued under the Bourbons. Louis XIV feared seeing the spire of Saint-Denis; his successors did everything for Saint-Cloud and Versailles. Today Saint-Germain still awaits the result of a promise which the war has perhaps prevented from being fulfilled.

III

A SINGING SOCIETY

The concierge took the most pleasure in showing me a series of small lodges that they call *the cells,* in which some of the penitentiary's soldiers sleep. These are genuine boudoirs, decorated with fresco paintings of landscapes. The bed is composed of a horsehair mattress, supported by elastics; all of it very clean and very smart, like a ship officer's cabin. Only there was no daylight, like the room offered to me in Paris — and no one could live there *having a condition* which demanded daylight. "I would prefer," I said to the sergeant, "a room less decorated and closer to some windows." — "When one gets up before dawn, it's really all the same!" he replied. I found this observation remarkably sound.

Back at the guardroom, I had only to thank the commander for his courtesy, and the sergeant refused to accept any buona mano. My idea for an English fund was still running through my head, and I wished to see what impression it might make on the town's inhabitants. So much so that, going to dine at the pavilion of Henry IV, where one can enjoy the most admirable view in France, a panorama spanning ten leagues, I presented it to three Englishmen and an Englishwoman who were delighted, Wnding this idea very in keeping with their national views. — What makes Saint-Germain special is that everyone knows each other there, people talk freely in the public establishments, and one can even converse with the English ladies without having to be introduced. One would be so bored otherwise! And then it is a population distinct from the others, with its own status, it is true, but a status based on entirely local criteria. An inhabitant of Saint-Germain rarely comes to Paris; some of them only make this journey once every ten years. Families from abroad also live there with the informality which exists in spa towns. And it is not the water, but the pure air that is sought in Saint-Germain. There are charming nursing homes, occupied by people in very good health, but weary of the buzzing and the insane bustle of the capital. The garrison, which once housed the guard, and which today houses the cuirassiers, might house as well some young beauties, daughters or widows, whom one meets on horseback or on the back of a donkey on the road to Loges or that to the Château du Val. — In the evening, the shops light up the Rue de Paris and the Rue au Pain; the people chat at the doorways, they laugh, they even sing. — The accent of their voices is very distinct from those of Paris; the girls have a pure and beautifully resonant voice, like in mountainous country. Passing through the Rue de l'Église, I heard singing emerge from the back of a little café. Many people were entering, women in particular. Crossing through the café, I found myself in a large room all decked with flags and garlands, with Masonic insignias and the customary inscriptions. — I had in the past belonged to the Joyeux and the Bergers de

Syracuse; I felt no discomfort, then, in introducing myself.

The committee was set up majestically under a canopy adorned with tri-color flags, and the president gave me the hearty salute which is given to a *visitor.* — I always recall that with the Bergers de Syracuse one generally opened the meeting with this toast: "To the Poles!... and to these ladies!" These days the Poles are somewhat forgotten. — Aside from this, I heard some extremely pretty songs at this gathering, but more than that, the ravishing voices of the women singing them. The Conservatoire has not dulled the radiance of these pure and natural intonations, of these trills borrowed from the warbling of the nightingale or of the blackbird, has not distorted with lessons in musical theory these throats so clear and so rich in melodiousness. How is it that these women sing so perfectly? And yet any professional musician could say to each one of them: "You do not know how to sing!"

Nothing is as entertaining as these songs which the young girls compose themselves, and which generally make allusion to the betrayals of men or to the caprices of the other sex. Sometimes there are gibes of local mockery which elude the outsider. Often a young man and a young woman sing together, answering each other like Daphnis and Chloe, like Myrtil and Sylvie. And with this thought, I found myself very moved, filled with emotion, as with a remembrance of youth... There is an age — the *change of life,* as they call it for women — when memories return so fiercely, when certain forgotten patterns reappear under the crumpled weft of life! One is not old enough to stop dreaming of love, one is no longer young enough to think always of pleasure. — This phrase, I admit, is a little *Directoire.* What brings it under my quill, is that I heard an old-fashioned young man who, having unhooked a guitar from the wall, performed admirably the old ballad of Garat:

> *Love's pleasure lasts but a moment*
> *Love's sorrow lasts an entire life!*

He had unbelievably curly hair, a white tie, a diamond pin on his jabot and rings with lover knots. His hands were white and slender, like those of an attractive woman. And, if I had been a woman, I would have loved him, in spite of his age: for his voice was deeply moving.

This good fellow reminded me of my father, who, when he was young, elegantly sang Italian arias on his return from Poland. He had lost his wife there, and could not keep from weeping as he accompanied himself on the guitar with the words of a love song which she had been fond of, and of which I have always remembered this passage:

> *Mamma mia, medicate*
> *Questa piaga, per pietà!*
> *Melicerto fu l'arciero*
> *Perchè pace in cor non ho...* *

Unfortunately, the guitar is nowadays replaced by the piano, as is the harp; those are gallantries and graces of another era. One must go to Saint-

---

*"O mother! Heal this wound, for pity's sake! Melicerto was the archer by whom I've lost the peace of my heart!"

Germain to rediscover the faded charms of the society of the past!

I came out under a lovely moonlight, imagining myself in 1827, the time when I had lived for a while in Saint-Germain. Among the young women present at this small celebration, I had recognized accentuated eyes, regular and, so to speak, classical features, characteristic intonations of the region which made me dream of my cousins, my girlfriends of this time, as if in another world I had recognized my first loves. I wandered by the moonlight through these drowsy streets and promenades. I marveled at the stately contours of the castle, I went to inhale the scent of the almost leafless trees at the edge of the forest, I savored more strongly at this hour the architecture of the church in which the wife of James II rests, and which resembles a Roman temple.* Around midnight, I went to knock at the door of a hotel in which several years ago I often spent the night. Impossible to awaken anyone. Oxen were quietly passing by, and their drovers were not able to inform me of anywhere to pass the night. Returning to the marketplace, I asked the sentry if he knew of a hotel which could accommodate a relatively belated Parisian. — "Go to the post," he replied, "they'll be able to tell you."

At the post, I met some young servicemen who said: — "That's difficult! They go to bed here at ten o'clock; but warm yourself a bit." They threw some wood into the stove; I started to talk about Africa and Asia. This interested them so much, that they woke up those who were sleeping to listen to me. I found myself singing Arabic and Greek songs, for the singing society had put me in this frame of mind. Around two o'clock, one of the soldiers

---

*The interior is today restored in the Byzantine style, and in the last several years they have begun to discover some remarkable frescos.

said to me: "You haven't minded camping out… If you like, find a place on a camp bed." They made me a bolster with a munition sack, I wrapped myself up in my coat and was getting ready for sleep, when the sergeant came in and said: "Where did they pick him up?"

"He speaks well," said one of the riflemen; "he was in Africa."

"If he was in Africa, that's different," said the sergeant; "but you sometimes let in characters that no one knows: it's not prudent… They could steal something!"

"It wouldn't be mattresses, at any rate!" I murmured.

"Don't pay any attention," one of the soldiers said to me: "it's his nature; and then, he just got some orders from *higher up*… that always makes him grumpy."

I slept extremely well until daybreak; and, thanking these good soldiers as well as the sergeant, who was altogether mollified, I headed for the hills of Mareil to admire the magnificence of the rising sun.

As I just said a short while ago — the years of my youth are coming back to me — and the sight of these beloved places recalls to me the sentiment of things past. Saint-Germain, Senlis and Dammartin are the three towns which, not far from Paris, correspond to my dearest memories. The recollection of old, dead relatives sadly joins the thought of several young girls whose love made me a poet, or whose scorn at times made me ironic and pensive. I learnt style through writing letters of tenderness or friendship, and, when I read again those which have been preserved, I recognize in them the clear stamp of my reading of those days, particularly of Diderot, Rousseau and Sénancour. What I have just said will explain the sentiment in which the following pages were written. I was regaining my love for Saint-Germain in those final beautiful days of autumn. I settled at the *Ange Gardien* and, in the intervals of my walks, sketched out some memories which I dare not entitle *Memoirs*, and which were instead conceived in accordance with the framework of the solitary walks of Jean-Jacques. I will end them in the very region in which I was raised, and in which he died.

IV

JUVENILIA

Chance has played such a strong role in my life, that I feel no amazement when I reflect upon the remarkable manner in which it presided over my birth. One could say that this is everyone's story. But not everyone has the opportunity to tell their story.

And if everyone did, there would be no great harm in that. Each person's experience is the treasure of all.

One day, a horse bolted from a green lawn which bordered the Aisne, and soon disappeared into the thickets; it reached the darkness of the trees and vanished into the forest of Compiègne. This took place around 1770.

A horse escaping through a forest is not an unusual occurrence. And yet my very existence rests on this event. One can believe this, at any rate, if one believes in what Hoffmann called the *sequence* of things.

At that time my grandfather was young. He had taken the horse from his father's stable, and after a short ride sat upon the riverbank, dreaming of I know not what, while the sun set into the crimson clouds of the Valois and Beauvoisis.

The water was turning green, shimmering with dark reflections; the redness of the sunset was streaked with purple. My grandfather, turning around to leave, could no longer find the horse which had brought him there. He searched for it in vain, calling out until night fell. He had to return to the farm.

He was of a quiet nature; he avoided any encounters, went up to his room and fell asleep, counting on providence and the animal's instinct, which could very well lead it back to the house.

This did not occur. The next morning, my grandfather came down from his room and entered the yard, where he encountered his father, who was pacing back and forth with great strides. He had already noticed that he was missing a horse in the stable. Sharing his son's quiet nature, he had not asked who the guilty party was; the culprit was plainly standing before him.

I do not know what then took place. An overly sharp reproach was no doubt the cause of my grandfather's sudden resolution. He went up to his room, packed some clothes into a bag, and, crossing the forest of Compiègne, he reached a small district between Ermenonville and Senlis, near the ponds of Châalis, formerly a Carlovingian residence. There lived one of his uncles who they say was descended from a Flemish painter of the seventeenth century. He lived in an ancient hunting lodge, today in ruins, which had once belonged to Marguerite de Valois. The neighboring field, surrounded by thickets which we call *the copses,* was on the site of an ancient Roman camp and retained the name of the tenth Caesar.[4] On it, one can harvest rye in the parts not covered in granite and heather. Sometimes while *burrowing,*[5] one came across Etruscan pots, medals, rusty swords or misshapen images of Celtic gods.

My grandfather helped the old man cultivate this field, and was rewarded in a patriarchal manner with his cousin's hand in marriage. I do not know exactly when this wedding took place, but as he married wearing his sword, and as my mother received the name of Marie-Antoinette along with that of Laurence, they were probably married a little before the Revolution. Today my grandfather rests with his wife and his youngest daughter in the middle of the field that he once cultivated. His eldest daughter is buried a long way from there, in cold Silesia, in the Polish Catholic cemetery of Glogow. She died at the age of twenty-five from the effects of the war, of a fever that she picked up while crossing a corpse-laden bridge on which her carriage nearly turned over. My father, forced to rejoin the army in Moscow, later lost her letters and jewelry in the waters of the Berezina.

I never saw my mother, her portraits were either lost or stolen; I only know that she resembled an engraving of that time period, executed in the style of Prud'hon or Fragonard, entitled *Modesty.* The fever of which she died has thrice taken hold of me, dividing my life into regular intervals. At these times, I always felt stricken with the images of mourning and desolation that had surrounded my cradle. The letters my mother wrote from the shores of the Baltic or the banks of the Spree or the Danube were so often read to me! My love of the marvelous and my taste for far-off journeys were probably the result of these early impressions, as well as of my long stay in that lonely countryside in the middle of the woods. Often handed over to the care of servants and farmers, I nourished my mind with strange beliefs, legends and old songs. An upbringing for a poet, but I am only a dreamer in prose.

I was seven years old and playing at my uncle's doorway, carefree, when three officers appeared before the house; the darkened gold of their uniforms shone weakly under their soldier's greatcoats. The first one embraced me with such effusion that I cried out: "Father!... you're hurting me!" On that day my destiny changed.

All three were returning from the siege at Strasbourg. The oldest one, rescued from the waves of the frozen Berezina, took me with him to teach me what they called my duties. I was at that point still a weak student, and his youngest brother's high spirits delighted me while I worked. A soldier serving under them decided to devote a part of his nights to me. He would wake me before dawn and take me for a walk over the neighboring hills of Paris, feeding me with bread and cream in the farmhouses or the dairies.

V

EARLY YEARS

A fateful hour tolled for France. Her hero, himself captive within a vast empire, wished to call together at the Champ de Mai the elite of his loyal heroes. I witnessed this sublime spectacle from the general's box. They distributed among the regiments standards decorated with golden eagles, forever now entrusted to the loyalty of all.

One evening on the city's largest square, I saw an immense decoration unwind which depicted a boat at sea. The vessel moved upon choppy waters and seemed to be sailing toward a tower which marked the shore. A violent squall ruined the effect of this entertainment. A sinister omen, foretelling the return of foreigners to the homeland.

The sons of the north returned, and once again the mares of the Ukraine gnawed at the bark of our gardens' trees. My sisters returned from the hamlet in full flight, like plaintive doves, and brought in their arms a turtledove with pink feet, which I loved like another sister.

One day, one of the lovely ladies visiting my father asked a small service of me: I had the misfortune to answer her with impatience. When I returned to the terrace, the turtledove had flown away.

I felt such grief, that I nearly died of a purpuric fever which drove all the blood from my heart to my skin. They tried to console me by giving me a young sapajou for a companion, brought back from America by a captain, a friend of my father. This pretty animal became my companion in play and in work.

I was studying Italian, Greek and Latin, German, Arabic and Persian, all at the same time. The *Pastor fido, Faust,* Ovid and Anacreon were my favorite poems and poets. My handwriting, cultivated with care, at times rivaled in its grace and emendation the most celebrated manuscripts of Iran. But I still needed Cupid to pierce my heart with one of his most burning arrows! This was released from the slender bow and dark brow of an ebony-eyed virgin, by the name of Héloïse. — I will return to her later.

I was always surrounded by young women; — one of them was my aunt; two women of the house, Jeannette and Fanchette, also showered me with care and attention. My child's smile evoked that of my mother, and the soft waves of my blond hair fell capriciously over the premature length of my forehead. I became taken with Fanchette, and I conceived the singular idea of making her my wife in accordance with the rites of our ancestors. I solemnized the wedding myself, performing the ceremony by means of an old dress of my grandmother's which I threw over my shoulders. A ribbon sequined with silver encircled my forehead, and I heightened the usual pallor of my cheeks with a thin layer of make-up. I called on as witness the god of our fathers and the Blessed Virgin whose image I possessed, and everyone indulged me in this innocent child's game.

I had grown, however; a ruby blood colored my cheeks; I liked breathing in the air of the deep forests. The leafy shades of Ermenonville, the solitudes of Morfontaine no longer held secrets for me. Two of my cousins lived around there. I was proud to accompany them through those old forests, which seemed like their domain.

In the evening, to entertain our elders, we performed the masterpieces of the poets, and our benevolent audience showered us with praise and crowns. A young, vivacious and spiritual girl named Louise shared in our triumphs; she was loved in this family, and represented to us the glory of the arts.

I took to dance very strongly. A mulatto named Major taught me the basic elements of both this art and that of music, while a portrait painter, named Mignard, provided me with drawing lessons. Mlle Nouvelle was the *star* of our dance hall. I came up against a rival in a good-looking young man named Provost. It was he that taught me in the dramatic art: together we performed short comedies, on which he would improvise with much humor. Mlle Nouvelle was naturally our leading actress and held the scales so evenly between the two of us, that we would sigh without hope... Poor Provost — since then he became an actor under the name of Raymond; he remembered his first endeavors, and started to compose extravaganzas, having for collaborators the Cogniard brothers. — He ended up very sadly by starting a quarrel with a stage manager of the Gaîté, whom he slapped in the face. Returning home, he thought bitterly over the repercussions of his imprudence, and the following night stabbed himself in the heart with a dagger.

VI

HÉLOÏSE

The pension in which I lived was in a neighborhood of young embroideresses. One of them, who was called the Creole, was the object of my first verses of love; her severe eye, the serene placidity of her Greek profile, reconciled me to the cold dignity of my studies; it was for her that I composed the versified translations of Horace's ode "To Tyndaris," and of a song by Byron, the refrain of which I translated thus:

> *Dis-moi jeune fille d'Athènes,*
> *Pourquoi m'as-tu ravi mon cœur!*[6]

Sometimes I would rise at daybreak and take the *** road, running and declaiming my verses in the midst of a pouring rain. The cruel one laughed at my fleeting love affairs and my sighs! It was for her that I composed the following piece, an imitation of a song by Thomas Moore:

> *Quand le plaisir brille en tes yeux*
> *Pleins de douceur et d'espérance...*[7]

I escape from these inconstant loves to recount my first sorrows. Not one cutting remark, not one impure sigh had ever sullied the homage which I paid my cousins. Héloïse, the first one, introduced me to grief. She had a kind old Italian for a governess who was informed of my love. This governess agreed with my father's servant to procure a meeting for us. They had me come down in secret to a room in which the face of Héloïse was portrayed by an immense painting. A silver pin pierced the thick knot of her ebony hair, and her chest glittered like that of a queen, spangled with braids of gold upon a background of silk and velvet. Overcome, in a fit of madness, I threw myself on my knees before the image; a door opened, Héloïse entered the room and looked at me with an amused expression. "Forgive me, queen," I exclaimed, "I thought I was Tasso at the feet of Eleanor, or loving Ovid at the feet of Julie!..."

She was unable to respond, and the two of us remained silent in the halflight. I did not dare kiss her hand, for it would have broken my heart. — O sorrows and regrets of my young, lost loves, how cruel your memories are! "Dying fevers of the human soul, why do you return to warm a heart which no longer beats?" Today, Héloïse is married; Fanchette, Sylvie and Adrienne are forever lost to me: — the world is deserted. Populated by ghosts with plaintive voices, it murmurs love songs upon the ruins of my nothingness... Even so, come back sweet images! I have loved so much, I have suffered so much! "A bird flying through the air told its secret to the grove, which in turn told it to the passing wind — and the plaintive waters repeated the supreme word: — Love! Love!"

VII

JOURNEY TO THE NORTH

Let the wind carry away these pages written in moments of fever or melancholy — it matters little: it has already scattered some, and I do not have the courage to write them over. As for memoirs, one never knows if the public even cares about them — and yet, I am one of those writers whose life clings intimately to the works which made them known. Moreover, isn't one, without even meaning to be, the subject of biographies, direct or disguised? Is it more modest to portray oneself in a novel under the name of Lélio, Octave or Arthur, or to betray one's most intimate emotions in a volume of poems? Forgive us these surges of personality, we who live in the public eye, and who, glorious or finished, are no longer able to profit from obscurity!

If I could do some good in passing, I would try to call some attention to those poor, neglected towns whose traffic and life the railroads have rerouted. They sit sadly on the debris of their past fortune, and fixate on themselves, casting a disenchanted eye upon the marvels of a civilization which condemns them or leaves them behind. Saint-Germain made me think of Senlis, and as it was a Tuesday, I took the omnibus from Pontoise, which only runs on market days. I like to bypass the railroads — and Alexandre Dumas, whom I accuse of having recently embroidered a little on my youthful indiscretions, spoke truthfully when he said that I had spent two hundred francs and eight days to go see him in Brussels, by the old Flanders road — all to spite the northern railroad.

No, I will never accept, whatever difficulties the terrain might offer, that one should travel eight leagues, or, if you like, thirty-two kilometers, to go to Poissy by avoiding Saint-Germain, and thirty leagues to go to Compiègne by avoiding Senlis. Only in France can one find such misshapen roads. While the Belgian road was built through twelve mountains to reach Spa, we were filled with admiration before the fluid windings of our main road, which follows turn by turn the curving beds of the Seine and the Oise, all in order to avoid one or two inclines of the old northern route.

Pontoise is also one of these towns situated up high, which please me by their patriarchal appearance, their promenades, their views and their preservation of certain customs which are no longer found anywhere else. They still play in the streets, they chat, in the evening they sing on their doorsteps; the restaurateurs are pastry cooks; one finds at their homes something of the family life; the streets with all their stairs are amusing to wander through; the promenade marked out upon the ancient towers overlooks the magnificent valley through which the Oise flows. Pretty women and beautiful children stroll there. Passing through, one discovers and envies everything in this little, peaceful world which exists on its own in its old houses, under its lovely trees, amidst these lovely sights and the pure air. The church is beautiful and perfectly preserved. A Parisian fabric store shines nearby, and its young ladies are lively and merry, like in *La Fiancée* by M. Scribe... What I find so charming in these little, somewhat forsaken towns, is that I recognize in them something of the Paris of my youth. The look of the houses, the structure of the shops, certain customs, some of the dresses... From this standpoint, if Saint-Germain recalls 1830, Pontoise recalls 1820; — I shall travel even further to rediscover my childhood and the memory of my parents.

This time I am grateful for the railroad — an hour at the most separates me from Saint-Leu: the course of the Oise, so calm and so green, carving out under the moonlight its small islets of poplars, the horizon festooned with hills and forests, the villages whose well-known names are called out at each station, the already noticeable accent of the countrymen who board from one distance to another, the young women with their heads covered in madras, in accordance with the custom of this province, all of this moves and charms me; I have the impression that I am inhaling another air; and, placing my foot upon the ground, I experience an even stronger emotion than that which overcame me a short while ago coming back across the Rhine: our ties to the land of our fathers are even stronger than those to the homeland.

I am very fond of Paris, where fate decreed my birth — but I could just as well have been born on a ship — and Paris, which bears in its coat of arms the *bari* or the mystic vessel of the Egyptians, does not have one hundred thousand true Parisians within its walls. A man of the south, who happens to marry a woman of the north, cannot produce a child with a lutetian nature. What does it matter, one might ask! But try asking the people of the province if being from such-and-such region is of any importance.

I do not know if these observations seem peculiar — seeking to study the others within myself, I feel that in one's attachment to the earth there is much familial love. This devotion attached to places is also part of the noble sentiment which joins us to the homeland. On the other hand, the towns and villages pridefully invest themselves with the illustriousness of their land. There is no more division or local jealousy, everything relates to the national center, and Paris is the focus of all these glories. You ask me why I am so fond of everyone in this region, where I recognize intonations well known from the past, where the old women have the features of those who cradled me in their arms, where the young men and women remind me of the companions of my early youth? An old man passes: I had the impression of seeing my grandfather; he speaks, I almost hear his voice; — this young person has the features of my aunt, who died at the age of twenty-five; a younger one reminds me of a slender country girl who loved me, and who called me her hubby — who was always dancing and singing, and who on Sunday, in the spring, would make wreaths out of daisies. What has become of her, poor Célénie, with whom I would roam through the Chantilly forest, and who was so frightened of gamekeepers and wolves!

VIII

CHANTILLY

There are the two towers of Saint-Leu. The village is above, separated by the railroad from the part which borders the Oise. We climb toward Chantilly skirting the solemn high hills of sandstone; then a bit of forest; the Nonette glitters in the meadows which border the last houses of the town. — The Nonette! One of the dear little rivers from which I caught crayfish; — on the other side of the forest flows its sister, the Thève, in which I nearly drowned from not wanting to look like a coward in front of little Célénie!

Célénie often appeared to me in my dreams as a water nymph, a naïve temptress; intoxicated with the scent of the meadows, wreathed in smallage and water lilies, revealing in her childish laugh, between her dimpled cheeks, the pearly teeth of a Germanic nix. And certainly, like her counterparts, the hem of her dress was often wet... I had to gather flowers for her at the marly edges of the ponds of Commelle, or among the rushes and osier beds which border the smallholdings of Coye. She loved the lonely grottos of the woods, the ruins of the old castles, the crumbling temples with their pillars festooned with ivy, the hall of the woodcutters, where she sang and recounted the old local legends: — Mme de Montfort, prisoner in her tower, who sometimes flew away in the form of a swan, and sometimes wriggled in the moats of her castle in the form of a beautiful golden fish; — the pastry cook's daughter, who brought cakes to the Count d'Ory and, when forced to pass the night at her lord's home, asked for his dagger to undo a knot in her shoelace and stabbed herself in the heart; — the red monks, who would abduct women, and hide them away in underground passages; — the lord of Pontarmé's daughter, in love with the handsome Lautrec, and locked up by her father for seven years, after which she dies; and the knight, returning from the crusade, unstitches her shroud of fine cloth with a sharp golden knife. She comes back to life, but as a bloodthirsty ghoul… Henry IV and Gabrielle, Biron and Marie de Loches, and who knows how many other stories dwelled in her memory! Saint Rieul speaking to the frogs, Saint Nicolas restoring to life the three little children chopped up into mincemeat by a butcher of Clermont-sur-Oise. Saint Leonard, Saint Loup and Saint Guy left behind in these districts a thousand testimonies of their saintliness and their miracles; Célénie would climb onto the rocks or onto the druidic dolmens, and recount them to the young shepherds. This little Velléda of the old country of the Sylvanectes has left me with memories which time revives. What has become of her? I will ask around at La Chapelle-en-Serval or Charlepont, or Montmélian… She had aunts everywhere, numerous cousins; how many dead among all of them, how many unfortunates there probably are in this region that had once been so happy!

At least Chantilly bears its poverty with dignity; like those impeccably mannered old gentlemen in white linen, it has this proud bearing which conceals the faded hat or the threadbare clothes… Everything is clean, orderly, prudent; voices reverberate in the resonant rooms. One notices everywhere the practice of respect, and the ceremony which had once reigned at the castle somewhat determines the relations among the placid inhabitants. It is full of old, retired servants walking disabled dogs — some of them now have the title of *maître*, and have taken on the venerable look of the old lords that they had served.

Chantilly is like a long street in Versailles. One must see it in the summer, under a splendid sun, bustling with lots of noise on this lovely resonant cobblestone. Everything there is prepared for the princely splendors and the privileged crowd of the chase. Nothing is stranger than this large gate which opens onto the castle lawn and which resembles a triumphal arch, in the same way that the neighboring building appears to be a basilica and is only a stable. There is something still there from the struggle of the Condés against the elder branch of the Bourbons. — It is the hunt which triumphs for want of war, and in which this family found glory again after Clio had torn out the pages of the great Condé's war-filled youth, as is depicted in the melancholic picture which he himself had painted.

What is the use now of seeing this emptied castle again, which no longer contains anything but the satirical cabinet of Watteau and the tragic, shadowy figure of the cook Vatel stabbing his heart in a fruit store! I much preferred listening to the sincere regrets of my landlady concerning this good prince de Condé, who is still the subject of local discussion. There is something in these sorts of towns similar to those circles of Dante's purgatory frozen in a single memory, and where the acts of a past life are relived in a narrower center.

"And what has become of your daughter who was so fair and happy," I ask her; "she married, no doubt?"

"Good heavens, yes, but later she died of a chest ailment..."

It goes without saying that this struck me more deeply than the memories of the prince de Condé. I had seen her in her youth, and I would certainly have loved her, if at that time my heart had not been occupied by another... And now I suddenly think of the German ballad: *The Landlady's Daughter,* and the three companions of whom one said: "Oh! If I had known her, how I would have loved her!" — and the second: "I knew you, and I loved you with all my heart!" — and the third: "I did not know you... but I love you and shall love you for an eternity!"

Another fair face turns pale, breaks off and falls, frozen, onto the horizon where the woods are bathed in a grey haze... I took the coach to Senlis which follows the course of the Nonette, passing through Saint-Firmin and Courteuil; we pass Saint-Leonard and its old chapel on the left, and I can already glimpse the tall steeple of the cathedral. To the left is the field of *Raines,* where Saint Rieul, interrupted by the frogs in one of his sermons, imposed silence upon them and, after he had finished, allowed only one to make itself heard from then on. There is something Eastern in this naïve legend and in this kindness of the saint who allowed at least one frog to voice the complaints of the others.

I felt an inexpressible joy traveling through the streets and alleyways of the old Roman town, still so celebrated for its sieges and its fights. "O poor town, how you are envied!" said Henry IV. — Today no one thinks of it, and its inhabitants seem to show little concern for the rest of the world. They live even more on their own than those of Saint-Germain. This hill with its ancient buildings towers proudly over its horizon of green meadows bordered with four forests: the shady masses of Halatte, Apremont, Pontarmé, and Ermenonville lie in the distance, dotted here and there with the ruins of abbeys and castles.

Passing before the gate of Reims, I came upon one of those enormous traveling carriages which roam from fair to fair, holding an entire family of entertainers, their equipment and their housing. It had begun to rain, and I was cordially offered shelter. The inside was immense, heated by a stove, lit by eight windows, and apparently housing six people comfortably enough. Two pretty girls were busy mending their sequined clothes, a woman who was still beautiful was cooking, and the head of the family was giving lessons in deportment to a nice-looking young man who was being taught how to play a lover's part. For this family did not restrict itself to performances of agility, but also acted comedy. They were often invited to the castles of the province, and they showed me several documents attesting to their talents, signed with illustrious names. One of the young girls began to declaim verses of an old comedy from at least the time of Montfleury, for the new repertoire was forbidden to them. They also act impromptu plays on scenarios in the Italian manner with a great ease in inventiveness and lines. Watching the two young girls, the one vivacious and dark-haired, the other, blond and merry, I began to think of Mignon and Philine in *Wilhelm Meister,* and then a Germanic daydream stole over me through the view of the woods and the ancient profile of Senlis. Why not stay in this wandering house if a Parisian home is not to be had? But there was no more time to act on these whims of green Bohemia; and I took leave of my hosts, for the rain had stopped.

$\mathcal{N} O \mathcal{T} E S$

NOTES TO AURÉLIA BY GEOFFREY WAGNER

The text used for this translation is the one established by Mlle Diane de Rossi (Genève: Éditions d'Art Albert Skira, 1944). It was collated with the text published in the "Bibliothèque de la Pléiade," *Œuvres,* eds. Albert Béguin and Jean Richer (Paris: Gallimard, 1952), which appeared during the course of this translation. [It has been collated by the current publisher with the new edition of the "Pléiade," *Œuvres complètes,* eds. Jean Guillaume and Claude Pichois (Paris: Gallimard, 1989). — ED.] Part I, comprising ten chapters and covering a period of approximately ten years, was published in *La Revue de Paris* for January 1st, 1855; Part II, covering only about two years, appeared in the same review for February 15th, 1855. Excellent English translations, of the emended Gautier/Houssaye text which Béguin/Richer do not accept, have been made by Richard Aldington (London: Chatto and Windus, 1932), and Vyvyan Holland (London: First Edition Club, 1933).

1   The two women are Marie Pleyel and Jenny Colon. The meeting between them, though, is thought to be apocryphal. Nerval met Marie Pleyel in his 1839-40 stay in Vienna (probably on December 22nd, 1839) after his liaison with Jenny of 1837-38, and it is Vienna that, at the end of *Aurélia,* provides the sinner with the key word *pardon.* Pierre Audiat shows that, if the meeting did take place, it is likely to have been in Brussels — *"dans une froide capitale du Nord,"* as *Pandora* puts it — which city Jenny visited at the time Nerval and Marie Pleyel were there, in order to perform in

Piquillo at the théâtre de la Monnaie. By a quirk of circumstance, "Adrienne" (Sophie de Feuchères) died in London on the very day of this première of *Piquillo* at Brussels.

2   Jules Janin gives a contemporary account of Nerval's hallucinated behavior here. Indeed Audiat, one of the most assiduous, and severe, critics of Nerval's work believes that Nerval actually used Janin's account when composing this episode of *Aurélia*. It should be said that there are several critics who feel that Nerval had little, if any, original imaginative ability, and they support their views by discoveries of this kind. The newcomer to Nerval, meanwhile, is advised to approach these questions of literary detection through the following general volume: Aristide Marie, *Gérard de Nerval. Le Poète — L'Homme*, (Paris: Librairie Hachette, 1914).

3   Nerval placed the ring on the "Brahma's hole" of Vedic literature.

4   The Elohim, the Hebrew God or Gods, are often mentioned by Nerval. An excess of intellectual curiosity, the longing to understand the divine mysteries, Faust's fault, means for Nerval not only an infidelity to the Christian religion, but also, by association, to Aurélia.

5   An incident probably borrowed from Hoffmann, whose cabalist Dapfühl files down a ring belonging to his daughter Annette, thereby producing thick black blood. Jenny's death, to which Nerval refers in the lines before this, was on June 5th, 1842.

6   Cf. Dante, *Paradiso,* Canto X, II. 37-39.

7   The word Nerval uses here is *"Ferouër,"* localizing his reference to the ancient Persians.

8   Nerval's "Père de l'Église" echoes Faust's famous remark:

> *Zwei Seelen wohnen, ach! in meiner Brust,*
> *Die eine will sich von der andern trennen...* (1, ii, 305-306)

(see *Pandora*, note 1).

9   This invocation by Nerval-Orpheus prepares us for the more chaotic world of the Second Part. Separated now from the society of mankind the poet enters the deepest regions of hell itself. The last words of *Aurélia* thus echo this invocation, which the severed head of Orpheus still uttered as it floated on the river Hebrus.

10   Probably the poet and translator of Dante, Antony Deschamps de Saint-Amand (1800-1869) who was also treated by Dr. Blanche.

11   Sylvie.

12   Georges Bell (Joachim Hounau) (1814-1899), a doctor's son from Pau, politically active in the 1848 revolution, to whom we are indebted for much editorial work connected with Nerval.

13   Heinrich Heine.

14   *Sylvie.*

15   According to Champfleury, Nerval took off his hat and threw it to the hippo. In a letter dated May 31, 1854, to Georges Bell, Nerval asks Bell to try to find the man he had struck (mentioned in the lines above) and to offer him *"une réparation."*

16   These delusions of grandeur, which occur throughout the poems, follow here

logically upon the moment of mystical pardon by the apparition, a moment of supreme reconciliation that proves too much for the poet. He is taken off to Dr. Émile Blanche at Passy (August, 1853).

17   *Le Journal des Débats* was founded after the 18 *brumaire* by Louis-François Bertin, and perpetuated by the Bertin family. After initial difficulties it became a noteworthy opposition organ until 1830 when it was involved, along with the *Globe National, Temps,* and *Constitutionnel,* in the revolution. For these papers were prohibited by a police order on Monday July 26th, the day after Charles X had signed ordinances at Saint-Cloud which amounted to a *coup d'état*. It was the issue of freedom of the press that first touched off disturbances. Monsieur Baude published his *Temps* on the Tuesday in defiance of the police order, his offices were broken up by the police, the discharged journeymen printers became turbulent, and barricades were flung up. *Le Journal des Débats* naturally became a staunch supporter of the July monarchy. Nerval probably had in mind here Bertin l'Aîné, who had a striking face and was painted by Ingres in 1832.

18   The picture of the Valkyries washing Nerval's body makes a typical purification ceremony that can be matched in both Dante and *Faust*.

19   Owing to this reference, early editors, like Gautier and Houssaye, felt invited to insert at this particular lacuna in the manuscript ten of the *Lettres d'Amour à Jenny Colon*. Many of these are fragmentary redactions, some apparently intended for another use than in the *Aurélia* by Nerval, although in another moment he seemed to have disliked the idea of their appearing before the public at all. In a case of this kind an editor, or translator, has to act as an interlocutor and, however sincerely previous editors may have felt they were serving Nerval by inserting these letters to Jenny here, Mlle de Rossi stands with those who have excised them. She is fully confirmed by

Béguin/Richer, who are fairly exhaustive in their paraphernalia and conclude, *"Mieux vaut laisser la lacune."* The text I translate, that of the original, is surely the one Nerval himself would have preferred in the circumstances. Not only is the artistic unity now undisturbed by this long interpolation, but we have a better balance in the manuscript, and one that reflects Nerval's intentions more faithfully. For suddenly to be confronted with a lengthy reminiscence of Jenny at this point overemphasizes what was for Nerval only one aspect of his womanhood creation in *Aurélia.* The letters to Jenny have frequently been published apart, and they can be consulted in the Béguin/Richer edition of the *Œuvres,* along with the rest of Nerval's *Correspondance.*

20   In the Deccan, supposedly the site of Aureng-zebe's tomb.

21   Audiat finds this idea borrowed from Cazotte's *Ollivier,* in a passage to which Nerval alludes in his preface to *Le Diable amoureux.* The point of noting this is to show that apparently not all Nerval's dreams in *Aurélia* were his own hallucinations, or, rather, that some of these dreams were as much literary memories as the play of his own imagination.

NOTES TO SYLVIE BY GEOFFREY WAGNER

The text used for this translation is the one established by Nicolas I. Popa, and published in *Œuvres complètes de Gérard de Nerval,* eds. Aristide Marie, Jules Marsan, and Edouard Champion (Paris: Librairie Ancienne Honoré Champion, 1931). I might perhaps add that the Béguin/Richer *Œuvres* reprints the text established by Popa, *"dont l'édition commentée est impeccable."* [It has also been collated by the current publisher with the new edition of the "Pléiade," see introductory note to *Aurélia* above. — ED.] *Sylvie* was first published in the *Revue des Deux Mondes* for August 15th, 1853. The first edition of *Les Filles du Feu,* the volume in which this story was collected, [together with *Octavie,*

Isis, and *les Chimères,* — ED.] was published in Paris by D. Giraud on August 16th, 1854; on October 7th of this same year Nerval signed over his author's rights to this volume to Michel Lévy.

1   The Variétés theater, where Jenny Colon sang between 1834 and 1835.

2   This sentence, more than any other, is the source of the expression "ivory tower." Thus it is interesting to find the phrase, often so loosely used, in the context Nerval gives it here, writing as he was in an era of rapidly increasing materialism.

3   The more austere scholarship of recent years has disallowed the possibility of this tournament. Although *Sylvie* was once taken to be topographically accurate, it has now been shown that Nerval gave himself considerable license with the facts of his beloved district. Place-names have been confused and dates rearranged. Flowers blossom out of season. Some of the walks Nerval takes in *Sylvie,* for instance, are of the order of forty kilometers over rough country, a sizeable feat for the young man to perform in the time allotted.

4   When Proust compared his "madeleine" episode with *Sylvie,* it is of suggestions like this that he must surely have been thinking.

5   The château at Mortefontaine corresponds exactly to Nerval's description here; see also the beginning of Section XI.

6   August 24th, the night of Saint Bartholomew's.

7   This section is a studied embellishment of Wattau's famous picture *L'Embarquement pour Cythère.*

8   Saint-Sulpice-du-Désert, pleasantly resuscitated and romanticized by Nerval, the grounds being in the ownership of Mme de Feuchères (Adrienne).

9   Auguste Lafontaine (1758-1831), a popular sentimental novelist of the time.

10   The Théâtre des Funambules was, as its name suggests, originally a vaudeville theater. It lasted from 1816 until 1862, and in 1830 began encouraging pantomime productions, especially fairy pantomimes such *Le Songe d'Or, l'Oeuf rouge et l'Oeuf blanc,* for which Deburau was chiefly responsible. Nodier, the author of *Le Songe d'Or,* Viard, and Champfleury wrote mimes for this theater, as did Nerval himself, for he would obviously delight in something of this sort. In 1862 the beautiful Boulevard du Temple, where the theater was situated, was pulled down by Haussmann.

11   In another story, *Angélique,* which precedes *Sylvie* in the collection, the reader has already learnt how Nerval's eye was seduced by this painter's rather glamorous frescoes for Hippolyte d'Este, who was Cardinal of Ferrara and from 1541 to 1572 Abbé of Châalis.

12   Nerval misquotes. The passage runs as follows: "No pure girl has read novels... She who, despite the title of this book, shall dare to read a single page of it, is lost..." (*"Jamais fille chaste n'a lu de romans... Celle qui, malgré ce titre, en osera lire une seule page, est une fille perdue..."*)

13   This would have been about 1834.

14   This building was indeed dedicated to Montaigne and it bore the names of Newton, Descartes, Voltaire, W. Penn, Montesquieu, and Rousseau.

15   Nicolas Porpora (1686-1766), an Italian composer of church music.

16   This was the Clos de Nerval, from which the poet took his name.

17   Sylvain appears in *Les Faux Saulniers* (1850), as the brother of Sylvie.

18   Apparently Pierre Lebrun's tragedy *Marie Stuart*, also attacked in 1840 by both Dumas and Gautier.

19   Nerval's projected drama of which he speaks here, *Francesco Colonna*, never reached the stage, but its worksheets have come down to us.

20   This drama again seems to have been abortive. Nerval also planned a drama on the death of Rousseau.

21   This is the Baronne de Feuchères.

22   Jean-Antoine Roucher (1745-1794), a minor poet of the eighteenth century and a victim of the Revolution.

NOTES TO ISIS BY MARC LOWENTHAL

It should be noted that *Isis* is a collage of texts. Despite his claim of having "visited the Orient with nothing but the memories, already hazy, of my classical education," Nerval supplemented his travels with extensive reading. He made strong use of a study by the German archeologist Carl August Böttiger entitled *"Die Isis-Vesper,"* a translated portion of which made up more than half of the first published version of *Isis* in a Fourierist journal in 1845. This portion was reduced over the next two appearances of this text, the third time being its inclusion in *Les Filles du Feu*. In this volume, this passage begins midway on p. 128 and continues to the end of section two. Whether it was Nerval who made the translation from German remains uncertain.

A passage from one of the final chapters of Apuleius's *The Golden Ass*, one of Nerval's favorite books, makes up the third through the fifth paragraphs of the fourth section. Nerval employed the 1822 translation by J.A. Maury.

The following footnotes correcting certain details in Nerval's text are provided by the new edition of the "Pléiade," (Paris: Gallimard, 1989).

1   Nerval means *Spurius*, not Scaurus.

2   Nerval means *Alcinoüs*, not Arsinoüs.

3   Nerval means to say *hypæthron*, not hypætron, in referring to a temple whose cella lacks a roof.

NOTES TO PANDORA BY MARC LOWENTHAL

Nerval had at one point intended to include *Pandora* in *Les Filles du Feu*, but the text was never published in its complete form during his life. For a long time it was known only as an incomplete confusion of fragments, until it was admirably reconstructed by Jean Guillaume in 1968. It is this version that appears in the newer "Pléiade," edited by Guillaume and Claude Pichois (Paris: Gallimard, 1989).

The earlier version of the text was known as *"La Pandora."* Some of the more significant variations between these two texts have been noted below.

1   Nerval's translation of the first part of Goethe's *Faust* in 1828 earned him an early fame, eliciting admiration from Goethe himself. The epigraph here has been translated from Nerval's own translation.

2   The following is a variation of the introductory paragraph:

MARIA-HILF

Here is what I wrote thirteen years ago. Let us walk again this road of grief and deceptive bliss. — I once saw in my childhood a remarkable sight. A man introduced himself on a stage and told the audience: "Here are twelve rifles: I beseech twelve ladies of the audience to load them, if they will, with gunpowder and to add to the load their golden wedding rings, all twelve of which I shall collect on the point of my sword." — This was done: twelve ladies fired at the heart of this man and the rings all slipped onto the point of his black sword.

Some fantastic apparitions followed this spectacle, images of subterranean gods. The theater was lined in red, and rose windows embedded with black diamonds shown forth to those gazing from the shadows.

3   The following is a variation of the preceding two lines:
I wept before the statues on the grassy slopes of Schönbrunn, in whom I saw my brother, and my mother and my great grandmother Maria Térésa!... Maria hilf! *Maria hilf!*

4   The following is a variation of the preceding two paragraphs:
A new love was already taking shape on the varying framework of two others. — Farewell, Saint-Germain forest, Marly woods, cherished solitudes! — And farewell, smoky town once named Lutèce, illuminated still with the sweet name of Aurélie — Amor y Roma! *Sacred palladium, forever engraved on the tomb of Artemis. I am of the blood of Hector and I escape once again: Æneadum genitrix hominum divumque voluptas...*

5   *A kiss from your rosy lips*
      And I fear neither storm nor cliff!

6   From the German *Fuchs,* a term designating a second-year student.

7   Marshal.

8   Fresh fish, seafood.

9   Vatel, a famous chef in his time, killed himself in the midst of a meal prepared for Louis XIV after finding himself unable to serve the main course of seafood on time.

10   In the French, "*...prétendait tissue de Golconde,*" apparently a pun on *issue,* alluding the fact that Biétry's cashmere was French.

11   The following paragraph followed in the earlier manuscript:
The story behind this hat would lead us too far afield. Be content to know that it had no other equal than that of my friend Honoré de Balzac. These were the two fattest hats in all Europe and perhaps the entire world. Aristotle would have made them the subject of an addition to his famous chapter, if he had been able to foresee their existence.

             But let us be silent: the tomb is the seal of mystery!
as the third fat hat said.

12   Mandate or money order.

13   The Rhine.

14   *Le Roman comique,* by Paul Scarron (1610-1660), had a considerable influence on Nerval. In this work, *Destin* and *Estoile* are lovers in a traveling troupe of actors.

15   *Pandora* has until recently been divided into two parts. When first published in the *Mousquetaire* in 1854, the printers lacked several portions of the text, including the ending. To fill up a lacuna, the following letter from Nerval to Alexandre Dumas, and the accompanying passage from *Les Amours de Vienne* was inserted, perhaps using the structure of Octavie as a model. The result was an incoherent series of events attributable to what critics claimed to be Nerval's state of anguish. Although the incoherence was effective in its own right, Nerval, even through the delirium of *Aurélia,* was never incoherent. Guillaume's reconstructed text now leaves this lengthy passage out:

I should explain that Pandora *follows the incidents I had published in the* Revue de Paris, *and reprinted in the introduction of my* Journey to the Orient, *under the title:* Les Amours de Vienne. *Personal reasons that I hope no longer exist had forced me to remove this chapter. If a little clarity is still needed, allow me to reprint for you the lines that once preceded this passage of my memoirs. I write mine under several forms, seeing it is the fashion these days. The following is a fragment of a private letter sent to Théophile Gautier, which only saw the light of day through an indiscretion of the Viennese police — whom I forgive — and it would take too long, and perhaps be too dangerous, to stress this point.*

Here is the passage that those interested may add to the first section of Pandora.

"Imagine a great fireplace of sculpted marble. Fireplaces are rare in Vienna, and hardly exist save in the palaces. The feet of the armchairs and divans are gilded. The console tables around the room are gilded; and the paneling. . . well, the paneling is also gilded. Everything there is, as you can see.

"In front of the fireplace, three charming ladies are seated: one is Viennese; of the other two, one is Italian, the other English. One of the three is the hostess. Of the men who are there, two are counts, another is a Hungarian prince, another is a minister, and the others are young men with a future. The ladies have among them their husbands and their avowed lovers, known to all; but you know that

lovers are generally accepted as the equivalent of husbands, which is to say, devoid of masculinity. This is an intelligent remark, think it over.

"Your friend finds himself then the only man in this gathering to judge from his position; the hostess aside (as is proper), your friend has a chance to fix his attention on the two ladies who remain, and this is even a little to his credit for the reasons I have just pointed out.

"Your friend has dined comfortably; he has drunk French and Hungarian wines, coffee, some liqueur; he is well dressed, his linen is of an exquisite finesse, his hair is silky and very lightly curled. Your friend is uttering paradoxes, something that has been stale for ten years back home, but which here is completely fresh. The foreign lords are not equipped to fight on this reliable terrain that we have turned over so much. Your friend is blazing and crackling; one touches him, he emerges with fire.

"Here, then, is a staid young man; he is tremendously pleasing to the ladies (we still say ladies, although in high society, it is in good taste to say women); the men are very charmed as well. The people of this country are so kind! Your friend passes then for a pleasant conversationalist. One complains that he speaks so little; but when he warms up, he is quite good!

"I will tell you that of the two ladies there is one who appeals to me very much and the other one very much as well. The Englishwoman, however, has a little way of speaking so sweetly, she is so nicely seated in her armchair; with such lovely blond hair with red highlights, her skin so white; some silk, some cotton and some tulle, some pearls and opals; it is difficult to tell what is in the middle of all that, but it is so nicely arranged!

"It is a type of beauty and charm that I am now beginning to understand; I am growing old. So much so that there I am the whole evening attending to this pretty woman in her armchair. The other appeared to be enjoying very much the conversation of an oldish gentleman who seems very taken with her and in the conditions of a Teutonic *patito,* which is not amusing. I chatted with the little blue lady; I attested with fire my admiration for the hair and complexion of blondes. The other, who was listening to us with one ear, abruptly leaves her suitor's conversation and joins in ours. I want to change the subject, but she had heard everything. I quickly try to establish a distinction for brunettes with white skin: she replies that hers is dark. . . . in such a way that your friend is reduced to making exceptions, conventions, protestations. So I assumed I had displeased the brunette very much. I was sorry about this, *for after all she is extraordinarily beautiful and extremely majestic in her white dress, resembling la Grisi in the first act of* Don Juan. *This recollection helped me, moreover, to fix things up a little. Two days later, I meet one of the aforementioned counts at the casino; we have dinner together, then go to a show. We become friendly with each other. The conversation falls on the two ladies I've spoken of above; he offers to introduce me to one of them: the dark one. I mention my previous blunder. He tells me that on the contrary that had been very well done. This man is profound."*

16   To "put on a pair of legs," meaning to run away at top speed.

17   The following is a variation of the preceding line:
I overcame her by desperately clinging to her horns, and I thought I recognized in her the haughty Mantis, empress of all Russia. I, myself, was the prince de Ligne — and she had no difficulty in granting me the Crimea, as well as the site of the ancient temple of Thoas. — I suddenly found myself luxuriously seated upon the throne of Stamboul.

The "Mantis" has several connotations: apart from the mating habits of the insect, she also represents Catherine II. The word itself derives from the Greek, meaning "prophetess."

NOTES TO WALKS AND MEMORIES BY MARC LOWENTHAL

Promenades et Souvenirs, along with *Aurélia,* was the last of Nerval's works. First published in three parts, the final section appeared only a few days after Nerval's burial at the end of January 1855.

The homelessness depicted is that which had been shared by many of those who had been uprooted by Haussman's plans for the city. The fact that Nerval was found hanging outside a night shelter (which apparently had not opened its door to him), adds a poignancy to these pages. Peregrinations through space and time, they evoke the mood and structure of *Sylvie,* while looking forward to such kindred walkers as Baudelaire and the Surrealists, or Robert Walser.

The following fragment dates from the time period of the *Promenades*. It was apparently discarded by Nerval, probably due to its indications of the time he had just spent recuperating from his breakdown (perhaps the "brief sojourn" he refers to at the beginning of the first chapter). The fragment displays a certain feverishness not to be found in the ensuing calm and control of the *Promenades*.

[PARIS - MORTEFONTAINE]

Glory to the tents of cedar and to the tabernacles of Zion! I recognized my homeland in heaven... The voices of my sisters were gentle and my Mother's Word resounded like pure crystal. Her voice no longer had the angry tone of the past, when I was hurled from Mount Olympus for having disobeyed the Lord. For a long time I rolled through space, hounded by the mocking imprecations of my brothers and sisters, and I fell with a heavy flight into the ponds of Châllepont. The marsh birds surrounded me, asking amongst themselves: what is this strange bird? Its feathers are a yellow down and its beak curves up like that of an eagle... What does it want of us, this stranger who has no altars nor homeland? Like the swans of Norway, he sings of a foreign country and of skies which are closed to us!

Yet it was among them, among the green groves and the shadowy forests, that I was able to grow in freedom. Muses of Morfontain and Ermenonville, have you retained my songs? At times your mad huntresses have aimed at me with a badly drawn arrow. I let my most beautiful feathers fall into the iridescent azure of your lakes, or the current of your rivers. The Nonette, the Oise and the Thève were the witnesses to my noisy play; I counted your granite peaks, your shady solitudes, your manors and your turrets — and those dark steeples which rise up to the sky like the spires of bones...

1   In French, an E-string, but also a live bird decoy.

2   The Greek should be Διόνυσος

3   Nerval is most likely referring to the Saint-Lazare station, whose address, however, remains to this day no. 108.

4   Nerval means the twelfth, *Nerva,* the land being the Clos de Nerval, from which Gérard Labrunie adopted his "ancestral" name.

5   *Traçant,* a dialect word for ploughing.

6   Byron's lines: *Maid of Athens, ere we part / Give, oh, give me back my heart!*

7   *When pleasure shines in thine eyes, / Full of gentleness and hope…* Nerval published the full poem elsewhere, prior to the *Promenades.* It is an assortment of Moore-inspired verses, drawing primarily from *Whene'er I see Those Smiling Eyes* and *Believe Me, if All Those Endearing Young Charms.*